Wolves Desires

Sam Dollar

Copyright © 2024 by Sam Dollar

All rights reserved.

No portion of this book may be reproduced in any form without written permission from the publisher or author, except as permitted by U.S. copyright law.

Contents

1. 01. — 1
2. 02. — 6
3. 03. — 11
4. 04. — 17
5. 05. — 22
6. 06. — 27
7. 07. — 32
8. 08. — 37
9. 09. — 42
10. 10. — 47
11. 11. — 52
12. 12. — 57
13. 13. — 62
14. 14. — 67
15. 15. — 72

16.	16.	78
17.	17.	83
18.	18.	88
19.	19.	93
20.	20.	98
21.	21.	103
22.	22.	109
23.	23.	114
24.	Epilogue.	119

01.

A Human's Desires. Train.

All my life I've depended on my family for just about anything, they've been there for me and taken care of me, and when Linden came into my life I knew I would be more okay, and that was true.

But at times I like to sit on my own and just think about the father I never had, the mother who didn't want me, and the boy I loved since I was thirteen who didn't end up being my mate, though life has given me so much, these are just thoughts that come to me without restriction.

I guess at times we do reflect on what could've been our lives if the people who were supposed to be there for us were actually there. I sigh trying to shove the negativity out of me, I had a nephew on the way and a mate now that I loved with all my heart.

I was blessed and I was grateful for it. "Hey babe, you okay?" I smile toward Andie as he comes to sit by our spot in the woods. "Yeah I'm okay, just needed air I guess, what have you been up to?" I reassured knowing I was okay with him close.

"Oh trying to avoid my sister and her friend, also getting this." He hands me a letter and I go through it with a smile. "Wait you got in?!" I asked standing up, he nods with watery eyes. "I did." He wraps his arms around my torso crying. "Its okay starfish, I've got you." I comforted him knowing he was crying his eyes out because he had lost hope of joining the Art program at Algiers.

"I'm so happy for you." I whispered in his ear and he chuckled sniffling a little more. "I'm proud of you, us." I add and he chuckles. "You know what this means right, we'll be going to Algiers together." He cheered and I picked him up.

"Yes, yes, yes!" I yelled twirling him around. "Put me down Train, you don't want to crush the best video competitor you have now do you." He chortled and I let him down. "Fine, but I'm still happy, have you told your parents?" I asked and his smile dropped.

"It's going to be okay." I comforted. "No it's not, they never support me or my dreams, they want me to do something else and I don't want to, I want to do art and follow my heart like I should, I don't know why they're so against me doing art when Amie gets to do what she wants." He exclaimed pacing around and I stopped him.

"What did I tell you about your parents?" I questioned and he smirked. "I should tell them to shove it, because I want to live my life, how I want it, where I want it, and with who I want." He recited and I placed a kiss on his forehead. "Exactly, you'll be okay, and if they won't accept you for you then I will be here for you, I will be your home okay." He nods wrapping his arms around me again.

My wolf felt content with him in my arms, I had mated with Andie but I never told him, and I blocked the mind link so he couldn't hear my voice in his head, I wanted him to be less stressed when I told him, and with one thing off the list and two more to go, the list wasn't that big anymore.

"I just wonder what they will do when they find out about us, we haven't exactly kept a low profile and I'm sure Amie is bound to tell them." He mumbled with his head buried in my abs. "I doubt they can do anything about it, I'm in love with you and you're in love with me that's what matters." He nods still hiding.

"Are you going to come up for air starfish?" I asked and he refused. "What if you drown down there, or find the sea monster?" I teased and he still refused. "I'm not scared of the sea monster, he plays nice half the time." He replied and I chuckled. "Oh really, does he?" I chortled. "Yes, plus you smell really good." I rolled my eyes at his addiction.

"Did you buy that gift for Linden?" He asked and I chuckled, the two had become close to each other more than Emric and I thought possible. At first, I had not liked Andie but when I realized he hadn't done anything wrong besides watch his sister and Charlotte bully Linden, then finally step away because he didn't want to hurt him, I forgave him bit by bit.

"No, but I will." I reassured and he scoffed. "You're dabbling I see." He nods and I snicker. "Don't pretend as if you don't like it when I multitask and help you remember things you easily forget." I groaned when he ran his hand over my cock and bit down on my nipple.

"Ah, ah, ah, we're not doing it for the third time in one day, starfish sex will only reduce your nervousness for a while, you just have to rip the bandaid off." He sighed and finally came up for air. "I guess you're right, let me do it sooner than later." He conceded and I held him for a moment longer.

"Let's enjoy nature for a while, then I drop you off at home." I ordered and we both sat down on the blanket, he took out his sketchbook and I began going through files Emric gave me. I wanted to help with the pack as much as I could since my best friend was pregnant and it also gave me experience in business management.

Though at times I feel inadequate and that I must repay the Everlins somehow for taking me as their own, I'm reminded that they didn't do it out of pity or the fact that mom couldn't have kids anymore, but because they loved me when no one else didn't and I'm always grateful for it.

After sitting in the woods with my mate for a while, I decided it was time to go, he had to face his parents about the whole issue of him being accepted into the Algiers Art Program, I was worried about him but even if I was worried I had to have faith in him to choose himself first and his dreams which I supported entirely.

"You sure you'll be okay?" I asked the worry evident in my voice. "I will be, it's time I finally took your advice, and I need to do this, for me, and if I'm not okay I will call you, okay." He reassured as he placed a kiss on my lips that I reluctantly let go. "Be careful." I warn and he winks at me before climbing out of the car.

I waited until he was safely inside and drove off, I knew Andie's parents were hard on him but not his sister which baffled me at times since the sister was the one who needed more taming than him and a life too, she never misses a chance to flirt with me and it's annoying.

I don't know what will get her to stop, maybe my mouth around her brother's cock, I snicker at the thought as I park inside the garage. As I'm locking the car the scent of Linden's brother hits me and my wolf growled audibly, we both hated Davey.

Walking into the house I began looking around to find my parents, they were with Linden's mother along with her rogue mate and son seated in the lounge. "Get out." I ordered and everyone seemed baffled by my order.

"Train honey calm down, they wanted to see Linden and I was hoping they would understand that he won't see them until he's ready." My mother conveys glaring at the three. "You can't keep me from my brother, I will get to see him." I scoffed looking at Davey.

"As far as Linden's concerned you're as good dead to him, now get out!" I growled loudly and they left hurriedly because my wolf was near. "I hate those people." I asserted and my mother chuckled.

"You're not the only one my boy, there is an alpha who requested for a meeting with us in three days, he claims we harbor his mate and I can't help feel Davey is involved." Dad exclaimed and I sighed knowing Linden was right about his brother, nothing good would come with him being back.

02.

Andrew.

I didn't know how to break the news to them, I didn't know what to tell them, all I knew was that I had to tell them and tell them fast before my sister could do it or any of my other family friends spilled by accident.

After Train left I sighed, not because I was holding my breath over his presence near my house but because he was my pillar of strength, he was always there for me to hold on if I needed to, he always put me first and I could always count on him being there.

Now I was alone and about to face two people I wasn't really ready to face, I had no idea what to do, and most certainly how to handle the obvious outburst they would have if they knew I was going to be majoring in art instead of business like they wanted.

I knew I had no choice but to do it and I would stick by my word to Train, I wouldn't let them define me, I had to take control on my own life. So I sighed heavily gathering my nerves as I walked further in to the house. "Andrew, come here, help me with this." My mother exclaimed from the kitchen and I groaned yet walked to her.

"Hold this, oh tell me, have you received the letter yet, or did you already take it from the mail?" She questions and I cursed lowly knowing this was her way of asking. "Uh, yeah I got the letter, I got accepted into the Art Program in Algiers." I mumbled lowly hoping she wouldn't catch on.

"Sorry what was that?" She asked sternly wanting me to speak up. "I got accepted into the art program at Algiers University, they have a full scholarship for my years there since my art pieces were the best out of all the candidates and they offered it to me." I blurted out everything and her fake smile fell.

"I don't think you understand what I mean Andrew, I meant did you get the letter to a university application you made for a real job." She harshly spat out and I sighed. "Mom this is a real job and it's what I want to do." I shot back making her angry.

"Not on my watch, your father and I didn't raise you to be some incompetent hobo living in a shabby apartment with nothing to go on because you decided to be an artist, hear me clearly you're not going, and I suggest you get your suits ready, your father will be taking you to the law firm so you can intern summer next year." She stated without room to argue and that's when I lost it.

"Enough mom!" I yelled back as the door closed and I let go of the pot she had me holding. "Andrew, why are you yelling at your mother like an idiot?" He questioned and I tried to calm down but I couldn't anymore. "I'm not going with dad to the firm, I'm going to Algiers and doing what I love, if you won't support me that's okay, that's why I have a scholarship covering everything." I let out harshly as I finally calmed down.

My father stood there shocked as was my mother. "First we allowed to be friends with that fag from the Ordells, now this, this is all he's doing isn't it, he convinced you to do this." I was baffled to hear my father accuse Linden of something he didn't do.

"This is not about Linden, this is about my future, and no one else influenced this idea, if you even paid attention to me you would know I have several paintings listed in the art museum of St Maine, I've loved art since I was a kid but you never took time to notice who your son actually was, you only barked orders for me to obey." I replied finding the defiance I needed in that moment.

"I said you're not going and that's final, your father will see to it that you're an intern at the firm and that's final, as for that Ordell boy, I don't want to see him anywhere near you, as well as that boy you've been running around with." My mother asserted and I scoffed.

"You have no right to impose anything on me, you've lost that right a long while ago, for once stop trying to control my life and check yours which is practically crumbling to pieces in front of you." I replied and my mother froze, I don't know how I felt a fist being hurled toward me but I dodged and threw my own.

When I realized it was my father groaning on the floor my mother gasped. "I'm not a punching bag either, you're not forcing me to do anything and that's final, I'm going to Algiers and deal with it." I finally spoke more calm than ever as my mother kneeled beside my father whom I had just punched.

"You've lost control Andrew, look what you did to your father, this isn't you, go upstairs you're grounded for the rest of the week." My mother ordered and I lifted my bag from the island. "Like I told you before mom, you don't get to give me orders any more, you're just a hypocrite." I took my bag and walked away.

I hated saying those words to my mother but I had had enough of all the things they had done to make me miserable, she and my father had turned everything I wanted around so it could suit them and their social standing, it was as if I was the pawn to their games, Amie was let off because for some reason my mother found no flaw with her.

Also for some reason hearing them call Linden a fag brought out my own anger, it just didn't apply to Linden it applied to me as well when she said it, I liked boys as well, hell I was in love with a boy, and I wanted nothing more than spending the rest of my life with him if he would have me.

Ever since I met Train my life changed, deep down I wanted him like a drug, every time I was around him the world ceased to exist, all I saw was him, I found myself again with him, he helped me get through my own depression after what happened with Linden these past few years, though high school was almost over I still had regrets about watching and not doing anything to help him, but now I was better, we were better and it was all thanks to him.

"Hey Siri play Billie Martin, Bird." I spoke and the song came on, somehow I could relate to the song as it was playing, I wanted nothing more than just to stay in that little bubble of peace before more tension arose between me and my family, I knew at some point my family would try lash out for my misbehavior.

It's funny how even though I punched my father so hard he fell, my hand was alright, no bruising in sight, the song stopped as Train was calling. "I'm coming up, I know you're not okay." He stated and I chuckled, he always knew when I was okay, he always knew I needed him.

He climbed the wall as inhumane as possible with the help of a tree I planted with Amie when we were five, silently he crept into my room. "Starfish, come here." He demanded and I immediately moved to wrap my arms around his torso. His smell and his amazingly large arms were comforting.

"There there, I'm here Starfish, I'm here don't worry." He whispered and I finally felt calm, he was all I needed to feel peace and be flooded with warmth I couldn't describe but be happy about. "I punched my dad." I mumbled hiding in his abs.

"I'm sure he deserved it." He replied making me chuckle. "Youll never like him will you?" I asked. "Not in this life or the next." He responded making me laugh. I was happy he was there to hold me.

+++

LMJ

03.

Train.

After comforting my mate and holding him till he slept I placed a kiss on his forehead and made my way to the window. "Goodnight starfish." I mumbled before jumping out the window and landing without a sound.

Andie and I didn't talk in detail about what happened to his parents, I already knew what happened since I opened the linked and probed into his mind to see and hear what he did, it's one of my packs abilities which is weird and cool at the same time.

So in knowing what happened, I went to him because I couldn't stand watching them treating my mate like that, I wanted to go over there and strangle them, but I realized I needed to be rational about it like Linden always told me.

So I let Andie be his own person and defend himself rather than I jump in and save him, Emric always reminds me that we can't always be there for our mates so they needed to fight for themselves at times and I believed he was right.

I loved Andie so much and I would do anything for him but I knew I had to let him face his parents and their abusive ways on his own without my help or he wouldn't come out of his shelf to be himself, today was a step in the right direction for that growth and I was proud.

I waved at the wolves in the distance who were on night patrol, ever since the rogues who followed us here showed up I suggested it was best to have constant alert and patrol on any people who came within pack territory and the town itself, with the help of my nerdy brother in law who is pregnant the system has helped greatly.

I sighed with a smile happy to have my life in balance and soon I would have my little nephew or nephews according to Linden, in my arms, I stupidly can't wait for them to come and spoil them rotten.

Thinking about it made me want my own family but I was going to take it slow, I only messed up once with Andie when I didn't wear a condom thankfully he didn't get pregnant and Linden gave him a shot in secret lying that it was a vitamin, to prevent pregnancy for a year which I appreciated because my wolf and I are sex crazed and my mate has the same appetite for it, weirdly enough.

As I walked further nearing home I began to think about what life could've been if I had met the father who plugged my mother and left, or the woman who didn't want me without even seeing me, I had made peace with it but they were thoughts that constantly came to mind when I thought about how blessed I was to have my mom and dad, along with Emric and Linden.

The wolves howled signaling the patrol change but when I sniffed the air I could barely make out Davey's scent and it made me angry. I pulled down my shorts and tore my tee-shirt off, with the small stretcher cable I always walked with, I tied the shorts to my leg and in one swift spin I shifted.

In a burst of speed, I was following the scent and the closer I got the stronger it got, I tracked the scent to the edge of the pack territory near Linden's old house but the scent moved past it due west, as the scent got stronger I caught the scent of blood in the air as well, I pushed harder and called for backup from the nearest patrol squad.

I could hear their heavy paws drumming on the forest floor as they came in my direction. "Surround them." I ordered and they did as told because as we got close I noticed Davey on the ground with a bleeding leg and three wolves.

"You thought you could run away huh, did you really think you could escape and leave him, you stupid weak little man." The wolf punched him so hard a tooth fell out of his mouth, I snickered in amazement and enjoyment of what they were doing, Davey needed more than just a punch though.

My squad was in position as was I. "Whose there?!" The man who had punched Davey yelled and I stepped out growling at the wolves who had come on our territory. "Fuck, they're probably going to kill us." I scoffed mentally knowing I wasn't going to do that but they were going into pack custody.

I shifted back and Davey didn't look ecstatic to see me and I scoffed, I had always suspected him of something bad and now I had all the witnesses and proof I needed to find out what the hell he had come back for. "Don't bother to run, you're surrounded, you're under arrest as well, by Ryeland Pack protocol, you're to be taken in for questioning as to why you trespassed into our lands." I stated and the wolves nodded without hesitation.

I knew the wolves had motive for what they did but wolves rarely did to humans what they did to Davey, and on top of that the wolves we had encountered were not rogues therefore Davey had a lot of talking to do, and a mess to clean up for himself.

"I don't know what kind of trouble you're in but I promise you, after this, you're gonna wish that you stayed away from my home." I growled toward Davey and I could see faint smiles on the wolves we had arrested.

"Emric we have prisoners and Davey, coming to the holding cells, it seems Davey has an explanation to give." I sent through the link to Emric and I heard him growl, he did not like Davey at all, and I knew whatever Davey had done his punishment was going to be severe.

We moved through the forest till we got to the holding cells, they were a bit of a distance from the packhouse, we normally didn't take in prisoners, they were used as punishment cells for rebellious teens and situations like these when we had to interrogate someone.

We kept walking and the wolves who guarded the holding cells came to us with clothes for those who didn't have any as we shifted, I wore my shorts and waited for Emric as he walked toward us. "Go back to patrol, we've got this handled." I ordered the wolves and Davey was dropped like a bag of bones in one of the cells, the other wolves were put in single separate cells with bars, not even wolf strength could bring down.

"I should be making myself comfortable on the couch my fiance made me sleep on so that I can wake up at two thirty in the morning to eat pickles and peanut butter with him, but noo, you just had to cause trouble and here I am." I shouldn't have laughed but I did, Emric's outburst though terrifying to everyone, to me it was the best joke of the day. Linden was putting him through hell but I knew he loved every minute of it.

"Now you, tell why the hell you were beating this piece of shit up." I asked one of the wolves and he walked closer to the bars. "My name is Smith, I'm from the Sunspear Pack, I was sent with my men to get our Luna back by any means necessary." His response shocked me and I started to piece everything together.

"The Sunspear is a small pack near West Harring City, close to the Drephair, but also in a two day distance from North City where Davey was." Emric spoke up first also piecing together everything. "By Luna do you mean, the current alpha is his mate?" I questioned and Smith nodded.

"I could never love him, he loves someone else, his parents are forcing him to be with me because they believe that these so called mates are important, bullshit." Davey croaked and Emric went over to his cell, the guard opened it for him. "Shut up!" He yelled and punched him, probably giving the guy a concussion.

He walked out and stood by me again with a smile. "He ran didn't he?" Emric questioned. "Yes, he wouldn't cooperate so we had to beat him up, we had failed numerous times to get him without alerting you, so we told our alpha and he's personally coming to get him by days end." Smith adds and I remembered the meeting dad had told me about.

"I know about the meeting." I spoke facing Emric and he sighed. "As alpha, I need to put pack safety first, though I may believe your story, I can't let you walk free until your alpha comes, therefore you will stay in custody but not in these cells, don't attempt to escape, my wolves will shoot you down before the first bone in your body shifts." Emric's words were cold and domineering, with his now 6'9 height, it was terrifying.

"Yes Alpha." Smith responds and I nod to the guards as we leave. "Sir what of the human." One of the wolves asked. "Leave him, just don't let him die." I replied walking out. "Sorry about this whole mess, I will get it handled, go to your mate." I asserted and Emric chuckled.

"I know you can handle it, but I'm not putting the whole burden on you, see you in the morning, tell me when you get home and rest, you're gonna need it." I nodded to my brother as he pulled me into a hug. "Love you Train, don't forget it and take care of yourself." I chuckled as he did what he always did when I was putting pressure on myself. "Love you too, Em."

+++

(I felt I brought out little of the relationship between Em and Train in the first book, so I guess this shows that even though the two aren't really biological brothers they love each other more because of it.)

LMJ

04.

Train.

"Hey babe, you look good." I kissed my mate before we walked out of the school main doors. "I feel great too, thanks for being there last night." He exclaimed and I hugged him. "I will always be there for you, even when you don't know it, I will always be there." I replied and he smiled.

"So I've got to get to work and then I have an extra class with Mr. Dalton the rest of the afternoon, I wish I could just hang out and play video games with you." He whined and I chuckled placing a kiss on top of his head. "I wish it was that simple but you need to save money as you told me not to spend more than a thousand on you." I added and he rolled his eyes.

"I want to be independent even if my boyfriend has thousands he never uses in his account, that's why we're both pursuing careers, plus save the money so we can get our own apartment during our college days, that's the plan, so no spending unnecessary money." He chastised and I grumbled but conceded. "Fine, as you wish starfish." He grinned as we walked to my car.

"I'm going to spend the afternoon baking with Linden, I miss his food." I stated proudly and Andie glared at me. "Don't rub it in my face that you're going to be eating all afternoon while I serve bratty teens and vain housewives." He asserted and I burst out laughing.

"It's not that bad, you get your own live Real housewives of St Maine." I chortle and he laughed as well. "I can never get over wigs and hair being pulled off heads and snide comments about how last season a dress is." He adds and we both laughed. "See not that bad, but I promise to keep some for you." I proclaimed and he kissed me.

"You're the best." He exclaimed as I parked in town village where the boutique he worked at was, it reminded of the day we got Linden his outfit which was the day I first met Andie and was intoxicated by him, it was funny how time had flown since them.

"Have fun babe, and remember, service with a smile." I chortled and he waved at me walking to the door, my phone buzzed and I checked to see a text from Andie. "The only service I give with a smile is to you on my knees." It read and I smirked looking out the window to the inside.

I mouthed an I love you to him and he blew me kisses before I turned on the car and drove off toward the packhouse, soon the alpha from the Sunspear Pack would arrive and I needed to hear what exactly he had to say about his runaway mate.

Also, I wanted to see my favorite brother with his huge belly, he could barely see his own feet now and was due next week since he would hit the sixth-month mark tomorrow, I had kept record of his pregnancy because Emric was horrible at it and with the pressure of running a pack I didn't blame him.

As I drove further in I noticed two SUVs in the driveway and I knew they were from the visiting alpha, hurriedly I got out of the car after I parked and waved at the kids going straight for the Alpha's office. "Train you've come just at the right time." Emric announced as I stood by the door before entering.

When I stepped in, tensions were high and I knew nothing good had happened in the room before I had gotten there, a freshly cleaned Davey sat by the end of the couch with his head low, a 6'3 alpha sat next to him, several wolves sat at their opposite among them was Smith, I was glad Linden had the office extended or it would've been suffocating.

"Good afternoon gentlemen." I greeted walking to stand behind the desk next to my brother. "Train please tell the alpha what happened last night as I've already explained to him of the events which happened when I first met Davey with my mate." Emric was stoic, seemingly annoyed which meant Davey had probably said something to be the cause, no one else but him.

I began to narrate everything that happened last night when I saw Smith decking Davey, what they told me, and what they told us both at the holding cells. "It's not true you're lying, I never told you he loved someone else." Smith and the rest of the wolves scoffed and so did Emric.

"Alpha Turner, tell me why your mate would run away, maybe sending him back with you might not be the best decision I might make." Emric stated and the alpha nodded in compliance. "I met Davey when he was with his friends hiking near our pack, as you know the mountains there have a beautiful view." Both Emric and I nodded because it was true and the alpha gestured for him to go on.

"I knew he was my mate then, so I pursued him for months, we started dating about five months later and I told him about what I was, he was accepting at first but he wanted to finish his studies, I moved to North City from my pack just to be with him, put my life on hold for him and when I thought everything was going great, I returned to check on my pack and family, since I was the next alpha but hadn't taken the title yet, when I came back to North City, I found his car and clothes gone along with a note that broke my heart." He concluded and everyone looked at Davey with disgust.

"I'm not going to argue with you to know if what you say is true, I know how despicable he is, but what do you intend to gain by getting him back, Alpha Turner." Emric questioned and I wanted to know too, Davey was cold that much I knew now, I didn't want to know his reasons for leaving the alpha because I knew they wouldn't justify what he did.

"I wanted him to be brought back so that I could sever our connection, I deserve love Alpha Everlin, and I know it's possible to find love with another, the Crescent Fall Alpha and Luna are testament to that, so I want to reject the man who won't love me because I'm a beast and nothing more." Alpha Turner asserted and my heart ached for him but I knew he had already made up his mind, I could see it in his eyes.

"Why?" I growled toward Davey. "Why do you always hurt people?" I demanded and he stayed silent. "I'm sorry but I just can't love you." He addressed Alpha Turner and I shook my head in disgust, I hated people like Davey, wolves and humans alike would kill to have someone love you and only you as long as you both shall live, someone you share a connection so deep that both your souls are halves of each other.

"Leave us." Emric ordered and the wolves except Davey, Alpha Turner, and myself stayed. "Proceed." I asserted and the alpha nodded. "I Jackson Turner, Alpha of the Sunspear pack reject you Davey Ordell as my mate and Luna." As he spoke those words he clutched his chest and dragged in a sharp breath, I felt sorry for Alpha Turner but even though they were mates it didn't mean he should tie himself to a man who would never love him.

"I Davey Ordell accept your rejection Alpha Jackson Turner." Davey responded and fell to his knees, such was the bond, it was painful to break but also freeing in their case. "Davey Ordell you're hereby banished from ever stepping foot on Ryeland pack territory, you may not be a wolf but the wolves will kill you on sight if you're seen near the pack." Emric announced and Davey was horrified.

Smith and the other wolves walked back in after Emric called them in. "Rest easy Alpha Turner, there are rooms waiting for you and your members, stay the night or a few days if you like." Emric added and Turner nodded gratefully. "Thank you." The alpha muttered and left.

"Get him out of my sight." Emric growled as wolves came and picked up Davey, going off with him to his house, I laid a hand on Emrics shoulder and he sighed. "At least we solved that." He mumbled.

+++

LMJ

05.

Train.

"These are the best, I could just swim in chocolate." I moaned to the choc chip cookies Linden had made with extra chocolate, they didn't taste like ordinary cookies at all. "Can I just have your recipe book?" I chortled and Linden rolled his eyes.

"No can do love, you see munchie over there would bury you nine feet under for taking his favorite thing in this very kitchen." Linden responded and we both burst out laughing. "So how you holding up with the whole Davey fiasco?" I questioned and he sighed.

"I don't know Train, Davey and I weren't and aren't the best of brothers, I could care less what happens to him but he endangered the pack and I just don't know how to wrap my head around that, I want him to be gone and stay gone, like before." He chuckled lightly as did I.

Linden had finally accepted the situation in his life that would never change, Davey had distanced himself so much that the two of them could be complete strangers, after the kidnapping he hasn't spoken to his mother at all and I wish it stayed that way, he was happy without all their drama and the pain they brought to him.

I wanted to be there for Linden, if ever they tried to hurt him again, he and I were the same, the people who were supposed to love us abandoned us, but we moved past it and now we are happier. "It's going to be okay, I know so, what we need to worry about is getting these two munchies out safely." He rubbed his belly with a smile.

"Oh they will come out just fine, plus I'm tired of having swollen feet, and eating the most bizarre food combinations." He asserted and I laughed as he did, I knew the pregnancy hadn't been easy on him since it was two little peanuts in there not one.

"Soon my dear, soon." I reassured as I cleaned up the kitchen and he went to sit down on the couch, Em was busy in his home office trying to catch up on work but I knew he wouldn't be long. "Oh I need your advice by the way." I exclaimed as I sat down on the couch next to him.

"What exactly do you want?" He cheerfully asked. "Date suggestions, I wanted to take Andie to something unique but I'm not sure where to take him." I added and he propped his feet on my lap, I began massaging them, they were too swollen for his own good. "That's nice, anyway Andie for the better part that I've known him had wanted to set the world ablaze with his art, take him to SandBury they have an absolutely amazing art museum, and cool restaurants." He suggested happily and I was already planning everything in my head.

"That would be great, I just need to plan how everything will go, but SandBury is a few days from here by car and I can't exactly book plane tickets now." I whined and Linden chuckled. "It will be like a road trip then, you get to have fun on the road there as well." He contended and I was tempted to agree.

"I'm sure he would love it, his home life has been a little rocky lately." I mumbled lowly. "Yeah his parents are conniving homophobic assholes, if I were him I would've ran away a long time ago, I'm just glad he has you now, and so it just makes my road trip idea even better, he gets to be away for a while." Linden explained and I finally felt compelled to accept the road trip idea.

Andie needed to get away, to breathe, though I knew it was only for a few days since I had to be there for the birth, I couldn't miss it. "But this road trip will only be a week, your due date it tomorrow, and the rest of the week should be your birthing, I am not missing the opportunity to see my brother as a mess." I teased and Linden burst out laughing.

"Oh it hurts but I can't stop laughing." He asserts as we both calmed down and sighed. "So all you need to do is tell him what you've got planned after you planned it, no one likes a man without a plan." Linden exclaimed and I rolled my eyes. "Did you plan to have kids?" I teased again and he glared at me.

"A nonregrettable mistake, this is the result of pleasure at it's finest and also the rewards of having a male alpha as your mate, you get a two for one deal, a man that's only yours and also the ability to have kids." He sassed back and we burst out laughing again, this was how it was with me and Linden, it was always laughter and happiness.

"How are my parents not here, they do know you're about to pop right." I questioned and Linden chuckled. "Emric told me they went shopping for the babies, I think it would be the 25th time they've gone shopping, Emma and Raz also came by and dropped tonnes of baby stuff too." He replied and I shook my head in disbelief, I knew my family and the beta family were all excited about the kids as I was.

The mention of my long time crush didn't affect me anymore, I had accepted the fact that he and I weren't meant to be and that I had gotten what was meant to be mine, a mate who had the same sexual appetite as myself, it was always stunning to see him always keeping up with the sea monster down below as he liked to call it.

"Have you told him yet?" Linden asked and I knew what he was asking. "No, I just don't want to stress him out right now, he's still has to deal with coming out to his parents and it's been hard for him." I replied to which Linden nodded. "It's okay, take your time, just don't take too long okay?" Linden adds and I nod in agreement.

I knew I had to tell him about me being a wolf, I feared his rejection, and also the pain that came with it, I didn't want him to be like Davey, to reject me because he couldn't see past my grey fur to who I was inside, not every human was as understanding as the one who I was sitting next to, he was a true gem and I hoped Andrew would love me too.

"Congratulations man, two more kids already, you're moving fast." We both turned to the sound of Emric's voice, both Linden and I wondered who had just had other kids. "Alpha please do tell us who had kids?" Linden asked and Emric failed to compose himself and I snorted at how easily Linden could make a 6'9 wolf disheveled.

"Its Marquee, he and Zavier now have twins." Emric explained and I wasn't surprised by the information, people in Marquee's family before they moved to SandBury had soccer teams for kids, no wonder he was carrying on the tradition.

My brother sat opposite me and Linden, he sighed tiredly and I chuckled at how content he seemed to be. "You staying for dinner?" He questioned and I realized I had a trip to plan and packing to do. "I wish I could, but mom probably left food for me at home and I need to plan my trip with Andie to SandBury we're going to set the world ablaze in paintings." I asserted and he chuckled.

"Alright, just don't literally set them ablaze and be careful, if you need any—." He added and I cut him off. "I know, I can always ask you, love you brother, love you too Linden, and you munchkins don't be trouble for your dad." I exclaimed in child like voice. "Bye Train." I made my way out knowing I needed to do a lot.

+++

LMJ

06.

Andrew.

"Okay this is going to sound rather random and ridiculous but I want to you keep an open mind, can you do that?" Linden asked as we sat outside, it was early morning and he had called making me rush over to his house so that he could explain, how in the world he got pregnant and why a wolf was stalking me at night.

I had known Train and Linden along with his brother were keeping secrets but I had a mind enough to know that I shouldn't go probing into those secrets, they would tell me when they were ready, I knew it was for the best and that had gotten me peace of mind so far, but now I was anxious about what exactly I was about to be told on the day my boyfriend and I were leaving for a road trip.

"I can keep an open mind Linden, just tell me." I asserted and he sighed. "Do you believe in wolves, or rather werewolves, mystic beings half man half wolf." He questioned and I didn't know how to reply, all I knew about wolves was that they were animals and they varied in size because there was a larger than a bear wolf which stalked me but never hurt me.

"I have to say that I don't believe in it because it's myth right, or maybe not, it's stuff made up in movies, something like that." I replied and he chuckled. "Well they are as real as you and I, only more civilized and more compassionate than us most of them." He added and I quirked a brow.

"Did someone slip you happy pills?" I teased and he glared at me. "What, I'm just asking because I don't know where this is all coming from." I explained and his glare softened. "Munchie would you please come here." He called out and a very large black wolf appeared from the woods near the house.

"Did that very large wolf respond to you?" I questioned and he chuckled. "He's more human than you think." Linden added and I was stuck on my seat paralyzed in fear. "Don't be afraid, he won't hurt you come." I helped Linden waddle to the wolf which seemed more like a teddy bear when I got close.

I kept my guard up but soon relaxed when I somehow felt warmth course through me when I looked in its eyes, I felt protected, strong, most of all safe, with nothing to ever worry about. I smiled when the feeling flooded in me and I never wanted anything more. "Still afraid?" Linden teased and I shook head to dismiss him.

"No I don't, is he—." Before I could finish the large beast stepped back and bit by bit fur became skin, I averted my eyes as beast became man with basketball shorts. "Wait a minute Emric!" I exclaimed in surprise, this was all too much and I started to panic. "It's okay, it's okay, breathe, breathe." Linden soothed and bit by bit I was calm.

"You're a man beast thing." I asserted and he chuckled. "I believe the politically correct term is werewolf." He mused and I was baffled, they had been wolves living in the woods, was my boyfriend one, was Linden one, I needed answers.

"Linden explain please before I freak out." I ordered and he sat down. "Werewolves are real, I was pretty much in your state when I found out too, they live here, it's their territory." He began explaining everything in detail, the packs, what happened when he met Emric, to his pregnancy which I was really ecstatic about, and about mates.

"So that bite mark near your neck is a mate mark?" I asked trailing my hand over the similar bite mark that was near my neck as well, fascination driving away fear. "Yes, you and Train are mates, two halves of one soul, you'll be together in this life and the next, he will never betray you, never love another and always be there for you." Each word he said had described how Train had been ever since I met him.

He protected me, he was always there to hold me when I didn't have the strength, he encouraged me to do things that no one did, he made me pursue my dream and never cared what anyone else told me, he was a dream come true.

"But why tell me this now Linden, why didn't Train do it himself." I asked and Emric sighed. "Fear, he's afraid you won't love him if you found out about us, afraid that you'll run from him in fear." Emric responded and I wanted to cry, I would never leave Train, I loved him more than words themselves, finding out he was something more than just a boyfriend made me the more happier to have him and love him.

"I'm assuming by your reaction, you would never." I nodded my head toward Linden. "I wouldn't, it's something I need to get used to but I would never leave him, I love him." I added knowing deep down each word I spoke I meant it. "Good, though I'm going to have to ask you to keep this to yourself until he's ready to tell you, can you do that?" Emric questioned and I understood why he had asked me to keep this secret.

Train had to be the one to tell me, Linden and Emric were just there to help me and guide me toward the light so that when Train finally told me

I wouldn't have a heart attack but rather accept him as both his wolf and the human, I desired both of him, I knew it was going to be hard keeping this secret but I had to, it was for the best.

"It's okay I won't tell him I know, thank you for telling me this Linden, Emric, thank you so much." I knew I could trust the two people in front of me with my life, they were special to me and they cared so much about Train and I that I felt inadequate for their love.

"We did it because Train does so much for us, and Andie I know how your family is like, I wanted to show you that you could always depend on your mate, always depend on us to be there for you and never leave you to suffer alone, alright." As Linden spoke I moved to hug him.

Besides Train, he and his fiancee were there for me, and I was grateful for their love and support, indeed I had people I could always rely on, knowing the woods were full of wolves that weren't out to kill me made me feel secure, it made living in St Maine a little more interesting for me and it saddened me that soon enough I would be leaving for college.

I would be back but it would still hurt leaving but that was something for another day. "Now that you know don't be a stranger, and when the time is right don't be hard on Train." Emric asserted and I chuckled moving back a little. "I won't, thank you, seems I need to hurry, I'm meeting my mate in about thirty minutes, see you later." I stated as I ran back to the front of the house.

The smile on my lips didn't fade, I was happy to know what I knew and that I had more than one person in my corner, I had a whole pack to turn to when everything was bad, as I ran home I felt peace deep down.

I quickly got inside, since I had already packed my bag, I showered quicker than ever and was done by the time by father came down for his coffee which I placed on the counter, he and I were on speaking terms but they had reservations. "I'm off." I announced hoisting my bag up to my shoulder and making my way out.

"Hey starfish, ready for the road?" Train asked standing by his car and I nodded happily, though I felt guilty about not telling him I knew, he had to tell me himself not anyone else. I smiled as we got on the road but didn't miss the glare from my sister. I wondered if she still wanted my mate, that felt really good to say, I would retaliate this time if she tried anything on my wolf.

+++

LMJ

07.

Andrew.

"The place was so beautiful and so inspiring, thank you for taking me there Train, I loved it and I love you." I confessed as we took a turn to the street where my house was. "I would do anything for you starfish, all you have to do is say the word." He replied making me blush.

I knew he meant what he said because I was his mate though I hadn't confessed that truth to him, I still knew it was true, he would do anything for me, and somehow in all that mix, I knew I would do anything for him to be happy as well. "You want me to stay with you for while?" He questioned but I knew he needed to get home..

He had been anxious about Linden having the twins without him, that at some point I called Linden just to confirm if he was okay, the concept of Linden's pregnancy he had disclosed to me but as something natural not involved with wolves at all, I didn't blame him for lying about it, he just didn't know how I would react to it, honestly, I would've done the same, omit the truth.

"No I had you all to myself for a whole week, I'm sure I can survive a night, plus you should be pretty worn out, we did drive for hours, so you need the rest." I responded and he chuckled lightly. "If you insist then, but call me, tell me if you're okay." He added though it was a given I was going to call him or text him before I slept.

"How do you feel about going on another amazing road trip, sometime in the future?" I asked and he quirked a brow. "I mean this one was fun, entertaining, informative, very very romantic, and everything else as sweet as you, so I just want to do it." I fumbled with my words and he chuckled again. "Babe I just told you, anything you want, I'm all yours." He expressed and I could feel an embarrassing blush creeping onto my cheeks.

Train and I had grown as a couple in the week that we were away, though I didn't know of his wolf side I realized what Linden said about him and his pack being more human than ordinary humans was true, he was kind, gentle, and loving, he was hot as hell and made my stomach flutter with his smile, and over time I was learning, he had the same goals and aspirations in life just like anybody else.

There wasn't a reason for me to fear him when I knew he wouldn't hurt me, he was the last person to hurt me, I was more likely to get hurt by my family than the werewolf I was bonded to and that made me feel secure in a very weird way, knowing I could depend on him to be my safety blanket when I needed one, I could depend on his love to always be there when no one else would love me.

"Starfish I love you, and you're tired, better get up there." He ordered and I had no reason to argue I had been drained physically but being with my mate I never really felt it, all I felt was him. "I will see you tomorrow at school." I mumbled with a yawn, I sighed afterward and he pulled me to him crashing his lips onto mine.

Vigorously he kissed me and naturally I submitted to him, I could never want anything else other than being underneath him or on my knees rocking his body in pleasure. A satisfied smile graced his lips after kissing me wildly.

I climbed out and he followed suit, handing me my bag, I kissed him again. "Bye, you horny man." I chortled and I turned to leave, he smacked my ass and leaned on the car to watch me strut away, I could feel his gaze on me till I slipped into the house.

"I love you." I mumbled to none in particular hoping he could hear me, I locked the door and made my way upstairs, I found my room the way I left it only that my laundry had been done which I knew was my mother's handiwork, it still baffled me that she tried when I didn't feel the love she was trying to portray by doing motherly duties.

I threw my bag on the floor and moved to put my phone and design tablet on the charger, as it turned on I started going through the several messages that had been sent to me over the week, most of them were from curators for my art or personal buyers which wasn't a surprise, I chuckled because of one photo Linden had sent me of him and Emric eating pickles and peanut butter in the middle of the night.

"So you're back." Amie hissed standing by the door and I whirled around to look at her with a quirked brow. "Yes, anything you need?" I questioned showing that I had no interest in talking to her. "So you've finally got balls, it's cute how hard you're trying when you know you'll never be anything without me." She stated and I scoffed.

"Wait without who —I didn't catch that." I replied and she seemed to be offended by my answer. "Listen sister, I never needed you, I will never need you, don't be so delusional as to think I'm one of the people who you trample on at school to get your way, okay, now beat it before I use you as a doormat, and next time, knock, your parents must have taught you manners." I retorted blankly and she seemed baffled by my response.

"You think you're so special, just because he's with you, he'll leave you after he sees how plain you are, you're nothing but a quick fuck to him, and when he realizes that, he'll leave you." She harshly replied and held an amused smirk. "You do know he's my boyfriend right, how many months have you been singing the same story but here we are and he's still with me, stop pining over a man whose taken sis, desperate doesn't suit you." I replied with a smile and her jaw dropped.

I banged the door in her face and turned away, Amie was always one to act better than I was, to be the golden child and it got to her head so much so that I became insignificant and she wanted to treat me like how our parents treated me and I silently took it, but now I realized I had been giving them the satisfaction of watching me fall and be their pawn.

I was starting to stand up for myself and no one would tell me otherwise because it was my life that I was living, no one would dictate it for me, I was taking me back and it felt really good, it was high time I became my own man.

Because I was exhausted physically and now emotionally, I decided to shower and go to bed, it was the best thing to do since tomorrow was a Monday and I absolutely hated Mondays, though if you asked Linden Everlin he would tell you Monday was the best day of the week and half the time when he said that, I wanted to strangle him.

"Hey babe, I'm okay, I hope you got home safe." I texted my mate and left the phone to go bath, the water was soothing, and my body felt so much better, it might have been fun but the driving part wasn't, sitting in one position for so many hours had cramping all over.

After showering I wore my pajamas and headed for bed. "I got home safe, though I think I broke my back starfish, might need a massage, I love you and good night my beautiful angel." I read it out loud and it still made me blush without meaning to, I locked my phone and left it to charge, my life was going great.

+++

Follow - Vote - Comment

LMJ

08.

Train.

"I love you and remember service with a smile." I kissed my boyfriend before he climbed out of the car with a smile. "You know how I offer my services and who I smile to, love you too babe." He mischievously replied by my window before walking away, I couldn't take my eyes off him, since the day I met him, he's always been intoxicating.

With Andie gone to work I decided to look around for baby clothes, though his due date had passed the doctor said he still had time, though any moment he would pop them peanuts out into the world, it was normal for Linden not to give birth right then.

I parked my car at the only spot I found unoccupied in village and headed to the nearest baby store I could find, it was kind of embarrassing how the ladies in the shop came swarming toward me to give advice on which ones to take and which ones not to. Though their advice was appreciated, I loved my starfish, he had the tools that make mine hard too.

I kept going through the rows and rows of clothes, twin sets mostly but keeping them gender neutral which was a term I learned from Linden, if you don't know what gender you're shopping for, keep it neutral. After what seemed like an hour I paid and got out, but that wasn't the end of my shopping spree, I was shopping for me as well.

If you tore through clothing as much as wolves did you'll need a lot more to replace the shreds that we make when we shift, even the boxers, that why I prefer to just go commando at times, save me the boxer I shred through when I shift.

I got into another clothing store and I was surprised to see they had the brand Emric and I always hunt for but could never find it, immediately I grabbed as many as I could and dropped them into the basket, another pile again making it three and I was starting to get weird looks, I wish they knew the struggle of shredded clothes.

After choosing my pile of boxers I moved to the clothing section in the store, I believed I was no longer shopping for myself, I was adding things for my alpha, it was probably the least I could do since he's by Linden's side three quarters and a fifth of the time.

I paid for everything and still got the weird looks when the cashier was checking my stuff, I glared at her and she blushed. I didn't feel the need to throw insults so I kept calm and classy took my shit and went on my fucking merry way.

Walking out onto the street I didn't expect to feel the presence of an alpha in St Maine, the only alphas in the city were Emric and dad, plus them being in the city meant they didn't get close to pack territory, but a guard must have seen them, or any other person who's from the pack.

I had a bad feeling about whoever was here, they were an alpha, but also rogue, and not alone, I immediately ran to my car with my bags, it wasn't far from the shop I was in, I unclocked the car threw in my bags without a care, locked it again and tracked the scent.

I kept turning corners, twisting and turning between streets and shops, it was a busy afternoon and the people were literally hard to maneuver through, when I passed pack members I waved but still kept running tracking the scent as it got stronger.

I finally came to a stop, it was a small diner, the one Emric took me and Linden for breakfast on days he didn't feel like cooking, I hated them in the place we loved and wanted them gone, I calmed my self and walked in, they couldn't recognize me because I was born to a human meaning my scent seemed human, not wolf.

I kept checking until I found the alpha, he was tall but not as tall as myself of Emric, my brother was a sky scrapper now with his height. I moved to where the alpha sat and tapped on the shoulder of one of the wolves he was with, they turned to look at me with their wolf eyes showing, a clear sign of dominance which my wolf didn't take kindly.

I growled back and they looked down in submission, live with two alphas your whole life, you tend to pick up on their dominating traits. "Move." I ordered and the alpha nodded to his wolves, they moved and I sat down where they were.

"Who are you and what are you doing in a city protected under the Ryeland pack." I growled and the alpha seemed to have realized where he was and from his facial expression, he seemed to know us. "I'm just here to collect someone that's all, he owes me something of value, I won't cause any trouble if he comes willingly, if not, my boys and I will wreak havoc." He threatened and I knew he wasn't joking.

"Listen, rogue, you don't get to threaten without concrete evidence of why you're threatening us, I would gladly slit your throat right here and make an example of you if don't show me why you're threatening my pack." I replied shocking him with my outburst and with our eye contact never faltering he knew I was serious too.

"You've got fire, I like that in a man." His tone changed and it became suggestive, I rolled my eyes knowing where he was getting at. "You're beautiful, anybody ever tell you that—." He paused waiting for my name which never came. "Quit stalling, and tell your puppy to stop texting and the one behind me to drop the knife he's not as stealthy as he thinks." I exclaimed shocking the alpha.

He scowled and nodded to his men, and I smirked, it was clear that these wolves weren't trained to hone their skills to be as sharp as they could be, to break your bones to the point where an SUV would run you over and you would stand and keep fighting. "Tell me what you want in my city rogue." I hissed and he threw his phone on the table.

"I had a deal with a bitch here called Davey Ordell, he was supposed to kill his mate for me, Turner, but he left the job undone, and on top of that I hear he rejected the alpha costing me my plans in the process." I couldn't comprehend all this new information, what had Davey gotten into these past years, what had he done.

"So he ran from you?" I questioned and the alpha burst out laughing. "Is that what he told you, he lied to you and your pack, before Davey found his mate Turner, I was with him, loved him, cared about him, and did everything I could for him, and he left me for an alpha until he realized he could never be anything for Turner, I mean have you seen Jackson Turner, I warned him that he could never match up to Jackson, but he was adamant and he left me." Though he seemed to be proud I could see the hurt in his eyes.

"He came crawling back and promised to do anything to regain my love, and I told him to kill his mate, the little thing couldn't go through it, he was weak and that's why he ran." The man explained baffling me with more animosity for Davey than ever, why did he have to play with people's lives. "So you want Davey?" I asked and the rogue ordered. "I want him, and if I don't get him back, your peaceful city will have bodies droppin." He responded with a glint of animosity and humor.

"Don't do anything because if you do, I will end you." I hissed and the alpha quirked a brow. "Youll get what you want, but if you touch a single wolf or human I will kill you myself and use your pelt as a bathroom mat." I didn't give him time to respond and walked out with rage boiling inside me.

+++

LMJ

09.

Train.

"Did you get all that?" I asked my brother through the link, I had opened it so that he could hear what I was hearing, though it took a lot of concentration it worked.

"Every word, I'm already at his house, he's not here though, he's near town village I'm tracking his phone." Emric replied and he sent me his location. It wasn't surprising that he was near me because I walked all the way across the city to where my car was parked in village.

"I've got him, we're both at town village, I'm bringing him to the packhouse." I asserted and closed the link with Emric, following his location I found Davey in one of the shops, it seemed I wasn't the only one in need of new boxers.

"We need to talk." I growled when I got near him. "What now Train." He groaned and I scoffed. "Come along Davey, you have a questioning to get to." I harshly grabbed his arm and yanked him forward, he tried to fight but it was useless. "We can do this the hard way." I punched him in the gut.

"Or the even painful harder way, which is knocking you out." I stated and he scowled whilst bent over.

"Now come on." He didn't fight anymore as I dragged him to my car. "Why are you doing this anyway?" He questioned seeming afraid. "Because Davey, an alpha, a rogue alpha wants you back, he's threatening to kill people if he doesn't get his precious bitch back." I retorted with a glare and he gulped down.

"No you're lying, he couldn't have found me, this is some sick joke right." He responded in almost a whine. "Nope, coffee brown eyes, mop of black hair, strong jawline with a scar." I described the alpha and Davey put a hand on my car to steady himself. "It's him, he's here, what's he going to do, fuck I'm not going with him!" He burst out and I slapped him.

"Listen here you idiotic bitch, I don't know what kind of issues you have or why you got involved with all these wolves, to begin with, but the obvious fact that stands right now, is that I'm not willing to risk my pack for your mistakes, I'm not doing that, he already told me about your deal, is that why you ran?" I grabbed him making him stand upright.

"I said is that why you ran?!" I growled and he shook his head. "Then why the fuck did you come back Davey, if it's not the reason why you ram from North City what is it?" I questioned my anger reaching its peak. "Because I couldn't kill him okay, I didn't want Turner dead even though I didn't love him and I wanted to be with Tai but he didn't want me back if I still had a connection with Turner." He explained and everything began to make sense.

I lunged for Davey and punched him again, I kept punching until his face was swollen. "Baby calm down, he's already half unconscious, I don't know what's going on but you need to calm down." Andie stopped me as the scent of the salty ocean hit my nostrils with soothing lavender richness, my wolf rumbled to the scent and we both calmed.

Though bloody I took Andie in my arms and kissed him. I groaned when he kissed back, forgetting we were in public, or I was beating up a man, he moaned and I grunted in our kiss as he easily submitted and I ravaged him, letting my anger go.

We finally pulled back and he was flushed, I smirked looking at my handiwork with his swollen lips. "I don't even want to know why you're beating him but I know it for a good reason, get him out of here, there's a scene now." He mumbled as a police car showed up but it was pack members inside.

"Put him in my car, clear out the scene." I ordered through the link as I unlocked the car. Andie just shook his head and turned to peck me on the lips. "Tell me everything when you have this all sorted out, right now it's more important." I was glad he didn't probe me for answers, I didn't know what I would say.

Davey came back to St Maine so that his alpha mate could reject him, when that rejection happened he knew Tai his former lover, a rogue, would come hunt for him as well to claim him back because he was no longer Turner's mate, it was a pretty good plan but he endangered my pack, and the city itself and that wasn't what we wanted.

"Okay I love you, and stay safe." We kissed again and he walked back to the boutique he worked at which was a few shops down the block. "We've cleared out everything sir, have a good day." I nodded to the wolves as they went back to the police car they came in and sped off.

I took off my shirt and wiped the blood away, though I regretted it immediately, one my mate wouldn't like me being half naked in the middle of the street for everyone to eyefuck me, and two the eyes that weighed on my body were too much, so I got into my car and drove off.

I needed to get the mastermind in the back of my car treated, after that he would be questioned and we would see what the alpha decides to do with him and his rogue boyfriend who threatened the pack, I wondered how Davey lived his life, constantly without peace, I always thought the reason why he left St Maine was because he couldn't handle being here.

Linden had said he was more his father's child than anyone else, and well Linden only knew him briefly but he grew up with an absentee mother besides that, I could understand his reason for leaving, we all process grief and loss differently but was his reason and processing right.

All that he did that's coming back to bite him in the ass, I wondered where it stemmed from, at one glance it was obvious he lacked affection and love, had he gone through all the shit he had, just to find someone who would understand him and love him or was it just a part of him that wanted the thrill of it all, he was blessed with a mate no other being could be better.

But as he claims, he couldn't love him, maybe he loved the rogue wolf Tai, for all his flaws and lack of anything remarkable in particular, maybe he loved him solely based on something they found to be mutual between them, even if he were to be cruel, Davey would still love him, devoted and loyal, it made sense in my head but could it be the whole truth.

Tai had to confirm it, even though he was a rogue alpha, had he fallen in love with a human, who found his mate but never let go, and had that human felt the pull to his mate but still held love for the rogue, maybe Davey wasn't as crazy as I thought, he had planned all of it and I was sure his end goal was being with Tai, even though the alpha rogue had nothing, he wanted him.

It was an endearing notion, I felt bad for all three men, Turner, Tai, and well a bit for Davey, the goddess had not only played poker with their lives she had moved to go fish right after, they were all a mess, but I knew I now had a solution that could fix it all.

I parked my car at the packhouse, took Davey in my arms, and walked to the infirmary. "Again?" The doctor inquired and I chuckled. "Yeah, he's not lucky." I replied making him chuckle and he gestured for me to lay Davey on the bed.

"I'll check up on him later, I need to report to the alpha." I explained and the doctor nodded in understanding. "He'll be out for a while anyway." He mumbled and I turned to leave, I had to tell Emric everything and my plan.

+++

LMJ

10.

Andrew.

I didn't know what to make of my mate's outburst, I didn't know if I should be wary of his temper if he were to actually go out of control would I be able to pull him back like I did today, everyone was watching but none would or could get close, it was a terrifying scene.

Despite the metallic scent of blood that lingered in the air, I didn't care much for it, I wasn't afraid of who was delivering those brutal punched, I was actually feeling sympathetic for him, in all honesty, Davey's return has been nothing but a pain in almost everyone's asses, the man couldn't stay gone.

He caused Linden and my mate who was striving to help the pack in Emric's place so much turmoil, Train had been trying to keep whatever problems he's brought away from poor pregnant Linden, who doesn't need any form of stress, but Davey being Davey can't seem to grasp the fact that he needs to go back to the hole he crawled out from.

I sighed shoving away the negativity that I was allowing to take over, I needed to be neutral in any case, I had my problems to deal with, which included my sister who for some reason is convinced my mate belongs to her, which amuses me to no end when her friend was recently dumped.

I for one knew Charlotte and Matt could never last, their circumstances weren't all that favorable, they were like oil paint on a bristled canvas with sticking out veneers, you can never make it work, no matter how hard you try. Though I saw it coming Amie hadn't and it was laughable when she tried to console Charlotte that it was Matt's fault, not hers.

Truthfully it was both their faults, but I'd gladly say good riddance to both, they were useless in my life or Linden's, literally trash human beings. "Hey you ready to go?!" The girl I worked with at the boutique called out and picked up my bag to leave, the bag was heavy with supplies I needed for the painting I was making for Train.

"I'm ready, we can go now." I responded and I followed her out to her car, today was one of the days Train didn't come to pick me up and I was slightly upset because of it, his beard and that goofy smile always made my evenings worth it, but thanks to Davey I was not getting that. "Thanks for the ride, Train was busy." I mumbled sitting beside her on the passenger side.

"It's cool, it's kinda sad your boyfriend is hot as fuck, I always look forward to ogling him, and that other tall brother of his, mmmh those are men right there." She confessed and my jaw hung loose. "What?!" I screeched and she waved me off like it was nothing. "Don't be weird, they're both gay I know, which is disappointing but I can't help ogle the eye fucking candy." As she defended I facepalmed.

Though I felt a tinge of jealousy it went away rather quickly, she knew he was gay obviously and her explanation made it innocent adoration, also for me it was kind of an ego booster, I was shamelessly proud to have a mate they wanted but never could get, he was all mine.

As we drove off toward my house the topic had changed to the lady who had her wig tossed away from her head when she got into a fight with another woman who was supposedly her husband's mistress, it was hilarious and one of the highlights of my afternoon.

"Well we're here." She announced and I turned to see we were indeed at my house. "Thank you so much for the ride, I will see you tomorrow at work." I spoke climbing out of the car. "You're welcome Andrew, it's the least I could do with that present you helped make for my mum, have a great evening." She called out and I waved her off..

"You too, and that was nothing but a pleasure!" I yelled as she sped off, with a honk of her car she was speeding off like a manic, I swear she killed a squirrel or two as she drove off. I turned to face the house that really no longer felt like home, I wanted the year to end so that I could say goodbye to it forever. "Only three weeks and a day till graduation, you'll survive." I mumbled to myself as I turned the knob.

The house was silent as always, but what caught my attention was my father and mother home, they were never home together, it was a miracle watching them sitting side by side, my father was a cheating scum bag and my mother knew it, but she did nothing because what would people say if she were to end her marriage, it was her status that mattered more.

The initial shock faded, I only nodded to them and proceeded to go upstairs. "Andrew, may we have a word with you?" My father spat and I knew nothing good was coming my way. "Yes." I responded lacking the acknowledgment he wanted. "Sit." He ordered and I rolled my eyes but obliged.

"Please tell me what happened this afternoon." That's when I knew I was screwed, well more a less depending on what they meant. "Nothing of interest." I responded and he scowled. "So the video of you kissing a man in village is nothing, you publicly showing off how you suck off another man was nothing, letting bloody hands roam your body is nothing!" He demanded but my emotions did not falter.

"Is this, what this talk is about because I don't need it." I asserted and my mother moved from her place on the kitchen island to slap me, it was as if I could see her moving slowly, I dodged and her hand hit one of the vases which shattered. I scoffed looking at her.

"You faggot!" She screeched with my father beside her. "What did I do wrong in grooming you, where did I go wrong as a parent, I didn't give birth to a faggot, I didn't give birth to this!" She cursed looking at me and a single tear fell down my cheek, I knew they would never accept me but hearing it now broke me.

"You didn't go wrong, and there is nothing bloody wrong with me just because I like men!" I defended and they both looked baffled by my response. "No son of mine will be another man's bitch, I won't let it happen in my home you hear me, Andrew, I won't." My father harshly grabbed my arm but his words had already numbed me.

"Now listen to me boy, this is my house, and I make the rules, since you won't listen to me when I told you to stop seeing that Ordell boy, now he's infected you with his disease, but no matte, I will give you two choices, live in my house and go to see a therapist who will help you get rid of the sick disease in you, let go of this art crap and become a dignified heterosexual man, if not, the second choice is to pack up leave my home this instant." I knew my option.

I didn't need to ponder it or maul it over, I knew my option, I immediately ran upstairs, I grabbed my bag which was already packed for this eventuality, grabbed the little things I still kept in my room and threw it all in my bag, I always knew I would get kicked out, it was a gut feeling for the past three years but now it was real, it's why three quarters of my stuff was in Linden's house, I had planned ahead.

"So this is what you've decided, but I won't let you get out that door without me at least trying to beat that sickness out of you." He sneered as both he and my mother stood at the top of the stairs. "No let me go!" I screamed when he grabbed me.

"Train help me!" I forced the link from my side, I didn't know if it would work, all I knew was that I had to try. My mother grabbed my pack tore through it, my supplies littered the floor and that made me angry. I pushed her back and she almost fell down the stairs, instead, my father grabbed her arm and I was the one the two pushed down the long stairs.

The first hit to my head drew blood, the second I felt my leg break, and I toppled over till I hit the ground and laid there feeling my blood flow, how had my day gone so bad. "Train." I mumbled as I fell unconscious.

+++

Follow - Vote - Comment

LMJ

11.

Train.

"So you think he planned all of this, it would make sense but we can't really be sure if that's the truth, it's just speculation for now Train." Emric reminded but I knew he believed every word that I had said, everything that I had speculated on about Davey was right.

He truly had no other motive, intention, or anything that would lead to a different conclusion therefore it was safe to say that he indeed planned for Turner to follow him and reject him, then Tai would follow and claim him, but why didn't Tai just track him down and go, he could've easily taken him and went on his fucking way.

"Its the only plausible theory and I'm all for it, let's wait for him to wake up and we'll see what to do from then on, I'm sure if I can reason with this Tai, I won't have to kill him." Emric concluded and I chuckled, it was easy for Emric to kill Tai, all he needed was a clear headshot and the wolf would drop dead.

"Fine if you think so, but as soon as he wakes up we're kicking him out." Emric nodded as I stood up to leave his office at the packhouse. In that instant, I felt pain radiate over my arm, but it wasn't mine therefore it was Andie, I opened the link immediately and his words had me running out of the office.

I needed to get to him I needed to help him, I knew he was home by now therefore when I got outside I didn't remove my clothes I just shifted and shredded them in the process, I ran at a full sprint headed for his house, my leg felt as if it was snapped, my head throbbed, all this pain wasn't mine so I pushed harder.

Wolves joined me as I ran toward my mates house, I didn't tell them the reason, they didn't need that reason, that's what the pack was about they would be there for you, no questions asked, no need for explanations. "Train faster I smell blood!" Emric zoomed right past me as he was bigger than me, his wolf was terrifying only one other alpha was as large as he was, Alpha Heathen.

His words weren't lost on me as I pushed harder, we made it there and we all shifted, the ten wolves that had followed me secured the perimeter, Emric and I wore shorts and ran into the house. "Train." I heard him mumble as his heart slowed down. "Andrew!" I yelled running toward the stairs, I held my mate as his blood trailed down his head.

"I'm here starfish, it's going to be okay." I mumbled taking him into my arms. "You, you're that man he was seen kissing, so you're his faggot boyfr—." He was cut off by Emric's huge fist, the man hit the wall and crumbled to the ground. "How dare you call my brother a faggot!" He growled shocking Andie's mother.

A car screeched outside. "Emric, Train!" I knew that voice all too well. "Mom!" I yelled in an almost agonizing howl, she ran in and gasp but immediately moved to check on Andie. "We need to get him to the pack doctor." Emric announced and my mother led us out as she tried to stop his bleeding.

"Go, I will keep guard here." Emric ordered and I couldn't dispute it, he was alpha and I needed to be with my starfish. Mom revved the car and made one hell of a one eighty with the car that shocked me, she pressed the gas and sped off toward the packhouse.

"I was driving toward the packhouse from West side, I saw you running here with your brother, so I followed, I didn't expect this, do you know what happened?" She questioned but I had no idea what happened, I was only early enough to make sure his parent didn't let him die.

"I don't know mom, I just found him by the stairs broken and bleeding." I tried to hold back the tears, to be strong but I couldn't, why did it have to happen to me, why Andrew, why was it always me that lost the people who love me, why did his parents have to hate him.

I sobbed pitifully until my mother parked haphazardly by the packhouse, the nurses were already outside the infirmary waiting for us. "Lay him here, we'll take care of him, and Train we need you closely, the bond you two share is what's keeping him from slipping into a coma." The doctor assessed as I stayed close to the gurney wheeling him into the surgery room.

"Wear these, stay close by the bed but leave room for us to move." I moved to a corner, stripped, and wore the blue sanitized clothing and scrubs, hairnet along with gloves and masks. The doctor came back as he was wearing his uniform for surgery. "Lets numb him first, inject the morphine, make sure his heart rate is stable." He instructed and I froze in place watching him work.

"He seemed to have taken a blow to his leg and head along with his arm." He spoke to himself as he operated on him, standard procedure would have me outside but with our bond, my healing was the only thing keeping him from slipping away.

"Head trauma, but damage has slowly started healing." He mumbled and I was relieved but still he removed splinters of wood from his body, they popped back his arm into place and his leg put back in its right position. The heart rate monitor spiked and I was terrified.

Please don't take him from me, please don't, please I beg you, I can't live without him, I can't do this without him, he's the love of my life please I beg of you. I fell to my knees begging silently with tears streaming down my cheeks, I couldn't bear watching my starfish leave me.

"Hurry!" The doctor yelled and I didn't look at was he was doing until the heart rate monitor was beeping normally again. "His pulse is back, stronger and stable, he's going to make it." The doctor had crouched down to face me and I nodded pitifully. He helped me stand as they wrapped my starfish in bandages.

"Morphine is circulating in his system plus the drug we injected for his sleep and his body to adjust to the fast rate of healing from your wolf, he should be fine." The doctor explained as we got out of the surgery room. "Train follow him to where they're taking him down the hall, it's crucial that you stay close to him for the next two to three hours." The doctor ordered as I wore my shorts over my boxers and nothing else.

I followed closely as the doctor explained to my mother about Andie's condition, she seemed relieved as I was but my wolf was not, he was counting the hours, he wanted revenge.

I stayed with Andrew in his bed for a few hours, it was night time when I groaned waking up, I felt exhausted as I lay next to my starfish, a blanket had been set on my body to keep me warm, it had the scent of my mother and it calmed me.

"I can walk on my own Emric, I want to see them!" I knew who that was, he was my best friend, my brother and the person I ran to when things got tough for me to handle, he smelt like home, the peace of it, rose infused with lilac on a summer evening, his scent was always calming and my wolf was eager to hug him.

Linden burst through the door, behind him my brother and our parents, they all seemed tired and distressed. "Oh honey, come here." I didn't need to hear that twice, I moved from the bed and wrapped my arms around Linden.

All my tears rushed back, the agony I felt when I almost lost him, I burrowed my head in his neck reveling in his scent. "I was so scared." I mumbled through my tears. "I'm so sorry sweetheart, but I'm here, I won't leave you to feel all this on your own." He always kept his promises, and as he held me I felt better, sure that I would be okay, we would be okay.

"Go get some air." He oreded, he was the luna and he could tell I wasn't okay neither was my wolf, I nodded not needing a verbal explanation of what he wanted me to do, I was going to make them pay for hurting him, so I ran out of the infirmary and shifted.

+++

LMJ

12.

Train.

I was angry, my wolf was angry and we needed blood, how could they do that to him, what did he ever do to deserve that, I knew Andie was standing up for himself but this had escalated to a point where I didn't understand how exactly they couldn't even fake remorse.

In my wolf form, I ran and ran until I stopped by the edge of the forest and looked at my starfish's house, hoping he would be by that window looking out with wonder at the large grey wolf in the woods but he wasn't there, he was at the infirmary because of them.

"I will kill you!" Though I yelled in my mind my wolf howled and my howl was answered, they knew my pain and sympathized with me and I wanted then to feel what he felt. I ran to the yard and shifted back, I wore the shorts I had tied to my leg and walked in. I found his mother cleaning up what seemed to be blood on the floor, his sister by her father's side without an ounce of remorse.

"You, what are you doing in my home?!" Andie's father yelled and I turned to face him with a blank face. "I wanted to know why you hurt him." I replied trying to keep myself calm. "That's none of your business, I'm glad he's gone from my house with his disease that you parade around like some trophy." He spat and that was the last straw for me.

"May I have his belongings please." I asked looking at the bags that had Andie's scent on them, I didn't wait for a reply just picked up his school bag and the other bigger one, I checked for his gadgets and anything that might be missing and carried it out, all the while they looked at me wearily, it was as if they were waiting for me to explode but I wasn't the one going to do that.

"Find my mother give her these." I ordered one of the wolves left by Emric to guard, he took Andie's things and began going back toward pack territory. Then I let my wolf take control when I shifted, he howled just by the woods, and the family with interest walked out to see.

Amie was the one to scream and run but her mother and father seemed to want to be brave, my wolf lunged for him, claws sunk into his skin ripping clothes and flesh off, he bit down on the man's legs thrashed him around until it dislocated.

They had to pay for what they did, I couldn't live without Andie, he was my mate, my dream come true and they wanted to ruin that for me, I wanted them to feel what I felt like watching him almost die in front of my eyes, they had wanted to take something precious of mine, I was going to take theirs instead.

Andie's father lay on the ground blood seeping from wounds and bites that I had inflicted on his body. "Please, please let me go, I don't know what you want beast, I don't know please I beg you!" He was begging, that was pathetic, when he was with his wife watching my starfish fall down those stairs why didn't he feel anything.

He stood there and watched him fall, blood covered his body and now he dares to beg. My wolf still kept on with his rampage, his wife lay on the ground, her clothes torn, blood seeping from bites and claws that had sunk into her skin. She wanted to be the center of attention this would suffice, my wolf sunk his claws onto her chest and dragged them from right to left, marred her legs with would, I crushed her legs and sure she screamed in pain.

We reveled in her screams, this was for my Starfish, they should feel what he felt, our paw hit the side of her head and she was knocked out. Mr. Krest, the man supposed to love and protect his children lay on the floor bleeding, with a broken leg and wounds all over his body I knew would be scars he could hide, he wanted to seem like he was perfect, in everything he did, but no one is perfect.

My wolf bit down on his right arm. "Please no, please no!" He screamed and I wondered why no one had come to help, even his own daughter, this is what they deserved for the pain they inflicted. My wolf kept crushing his arm, breaking skin and bone, blood splashed everywhere until I snapped it off, showing broken bone and blood.

He would no longer hurt anybody else, I had taken that from him, he wouldn't hurt anyone else I made sure of it. I howled until the daughter walked out and screamed looking at her parents, I was by the forest line again but my wolf wasn't satisfied, so with a burst of speed, we lunged for the girl.

She had treated Linden like he didn't matter, abused him with her trash, faked friendship with him only to use him, she was cruel just like her parents, my wolf slashed at her body, claw after claw until her dress was stained with blood, she deserved this as well, she had also abused my starfish, her own twin.

Rage bubbled up again as my wolf thrashed the screaming girl until I felt the snap of her leg and claws dripping her blood. "Peanut it's okay, it's enough, come to me, it's okay." I couldn't see him near me but I knew it was Linden, he had followed me here, he promised to be here for me, but he was pregnant he couldn't be out like this.

I tossed aside Amie's body and made a dash for the tree line, Linden, Emric and my parent were all there, my wolf had given back control. "Call an ambulance for them." Emric ordered the wolf next to him. "Yes Alpha." He replied and left. "Don't ever do that again, oh I swear to the goddess I will beat you myself!" Linden yelled and both my wolf and I whined, we hated it when he was angry..

."Look what you had me do, he couldn't stay in the hospital knowing you weren't there, he promised to be by your side, now we've tracked you here and he won't listen, you're the only one he's fully concerned about right now, as am I but he's pregnant, so please for the love of munchie let's go home." Emric chastised and I whined again.

"I'm sorry." I responded through the link and Linden sighed. "It's fine, but when these two are born you're going to be babysitting till you leave for college, on breaks you'll be babysitting, until you finish college, that's your punishment." I could live with that but I didn't miss the proud note in his voice.

"Let's go home and you get cleaned up you look like a rabid animal." Dad finally spoke up and I glared at him. "You know it's the truth." He retorted and I looked at my fur all bloody, it was indeed gross. "Dad get these two home, I need to clean that up." Emric ordered and our father obliged. He kissed his mate and his stomach before walking off to the Krest house.

"Come on let's go." My father urged as he took pregnant Linden into his arms and I walked beside mom who despite the blood that covered my fur brushed her hand through it. "You look kind of roguish, it suits you." She commented through the link. "Mom!" I whined and she burst into a fit of giggles.

"I'm telling you the truth, I'm your mother, after all, you better believe me, Andie seems to like the bad boy, don't you think." She kept on and I was glad to be in wolf form, my blush was covered by fur. "You're blushing, that's even more cute, bashful, and shy." She added and I whined again.

"Dad, mom is making fun of me, tell her I look wolf hot, she says I'm cute." I whined and dad burst out laughing. "I think she's right, she's your mother and she knows best." He defended but embarrassing as it was I loved my mother and father, no matter what I did they would always love me and support me.

+++

LMJ

13.

Andrew.

"No let me go!" Those were the first words that rung out in my head, I didn't know what happened after, it was a hazy memory but I could feel it in my bones literally, I fell down the stairs, I broke my leg, I hit my head then nothing.

The memories were playing out in my head like a movie, I wondered what my father thought would happen when he said he would beat the gay out of me, was I supposed to feel differently, to love differently, or rather be a different person altogether, would it even make sense though, conversion therapy has one in hundred chances of working.

So maybe he thought he would apply it on me and have results, I chuckled bitterly to the thought, how could he easily push me over, easily let me go, and not feel an ounce of guilt, was I even worth anything to my parents now that they knew I was gay, would it even matter anyway, I hated them, and I wished karma the old hag would visit them.

My hatred stemmed from a lot of things, my childhood, up until now was orchestrated by them, I did everything they wanted and for once when I didn't do what they wanted, when I chose to follow my own heart and love who I wanted they tossed me to the side because I wasn't the chess piece anymore.

.It hurt deeply but I couldn't do anything about it, I was too powerless for it, the only thing I wanted was to just be in my mates arms and hold on to him for support, for reassurance that life would get better, for the love I knew he always had for me, that's all I wanted and nothing more.

"Hey sweetheart how you feeling?" The voice in my head spoke and it creeped me out, I could hear Mrs. Everlin in my head. I began to recall what Linden told me about the pack, a mind link was in place that connected everyone who was part of the pack, but how was I part of it. "You're Train's mate, sweetie, remember that." She reminded and I mentally facepalmed.

If I could hear her did it mean I was awake, had I survived my fall, and where was I, I began to panic, I wanted to know where I was if only I could open my eyes and see where I was, why was it so hard. "Andie calm down baby, calm down sweetheart, the doctor is removing the bandages don't worry calm down." Mrs. Everlin soothed me like a mother.

Was that how it felt to have a mother care for you, did it feel warm and protective, did it make your insides warm and fuzzy, like you could depend on her to be there, to love you unconditionally, that's how I felt like when she calmed me down, I felt safe and perfectly okay like she would chase the bad things that haunted me away.

"Where am I?" I focused my thought on Mrs. Everlin. "The pack infirmary, the doctor is just about done so don't fret." She replied and I waited as I felt the weight lift from my eyes, I opened them all too soon, my senses were overwhelmed. It was too bright, so I closed my eyes and groaned looking to the side.

"Lex darling close the shutters." She spoke sweetly to her husband. "Yes, dear." Mr. Everlin replied and they reminded me of Linden and Emric, they were always so loving and caring, it was sickeningly sweet and I loved every moment of it because Train and I were sickeningly sweet as well.

Where was he, where is my mate, I called out to him, he had come to rescue me that was obvious since I was at the pack infirmary, but then shouldn't he be by my side. "Train." I mumbled through the link focusing on him but it seemed I couldn't get through, did he close our link again.

"Train?" I directed my thoughts to Mrs. Everlin and she smiled. "He's asleep in the next room honey, he was restless and tried to keep himself up but between healing you and all that happened, well it caught up to him so he's sleeping." Her response made little sense, how was he tired from healing me.

"What do you mean, healing me, and what happened?" I questioned looking at Mr. Everlin who smiled making me blush, he was just as beautiful as his sons, damn come to think of it the Everlin family was a seriously beautiful family Linden included, he looked like a supermodel, I mentally banged my head for going off-topic.

"Oh don't worry Train will tell you when he wakes up, but why don't we talk about wolves, do you know anything?" Mr. Everlin asked looking charming as always.   "Yes I do know, Linden and Emric told me and gave me through wolf 101, and I read everything from the books he gave me, this is Ryeland Pack territory." I replied through the link feeling proud of myself for learning and also because my throat was dry.

"Well it seems the boys got you educated on wolves then, thank the Goddess for that because the speech about wolves is long and hard and honestly boring if the person decides to panic and faint over and over again, really stressful stuff." Mr. Everlin rambled on making me smile and his mate chuckle.

"It's okay sweetheart, I know." Mrs. Everlin placed a kiss on his cheek, they were so in love it was practically rolling off them. "What I meant by healing you, it's more of a connection between the two of you, honey you had a broken leg and well you hit your head several times on the stairs causing major damage to your head, the fall you had would've resulted in you being in a coma or death." She sighed and I knew she was trying to get rid of the thoughts of death.

"But luckily you called out just in time for Train to hear you and come rescue you, though you had already fallen the healing kicked in quickly because he was close to you, what I'm trying to say is, Train is a wolf right, he heals at an astonishing rate, you being human well you heal at a slower pace, when you mated with Train, yeah the whole process, you share his healing and reflexes, and at times more but it depends on the mates most of the time." She explained and everything suddenly made sense.

"So he's drained and asleep because he's healing me, my leg and my head, almost all my injuries " I questioned and she nodded. "Yeah, it's why your leg has already healed halfway through, you just need to stay off it for a day or two for it to completely heal, plus with the surgery, you underwent the doctor confirmed that your head was already healing by the time they finished." Mr. Everlin was the one who responded shocking me but it was true.

My body was sore that was for sure but my head was perfectly fine, and when I should've felt pain, it wasn't there, tears began to well up in my eyes as I remembered why I was in that bed, and why I didn't feel pain, Train had rescued me from my parents who didn't care about me and now he was taking my pain away, I felt undeserving of his love.

He had been through so much and here I was adding more to the pile, I didn't want to hurt him anymore, I loved him, I truly loved him, and him taking the pain I was supposed to feel made me feel so guilty. We were supposed to share this pain, he wasn't supposed to take it all on himself, that's what mates did, they shared in everything.

"Oh, honey." Mrs. Everlin hugged me from the bed and I let out all my pain and fear, the fear of never seeing Train again, of never seeing Linden and his kids, the fear of not growing old with the man I loved, I had felt that fear rolling down the stairs but now I was safe, I was okay and all I wanted more than anything was Train.

+++

LMJ

14.

The most valuable thing we have is truth.Brotherly Bonding.

Train.

After going back to the infirmary I barely made it to Andie's room before I fell to the floor exhausted, I wasn't really surprised by my sudden collapse, I knew it was bound to happen, dad helped me to the next room, cleaned up and I fell asleep.

I groaned moving to the side to avoid the sunlight streaming into the room, it was too early to wake up, or was it me who was just feeling lazy, so I groaned again when it seemed the sunlight was intensifying. "Mom I'm trying to sleep." I mumbled and a low chuckle rung out in the room.

"Mom is not here and you've slept half the day away, come on wake up." It was Emric who spoke adjusting the blinds and laying next to me, I immediately tangled myself with his body and sighed to the comfort. It reminded me of the days when we were young and I would have nightmares, I would cling to my brother and his scent always made me feel better, he always felt safe.

"Ah, I see you're being a baby all over again." He teased and I whined with my head on his chest. "Yes I fucking feel like being a baby right now, I'm scared." I confessed how I felt then, Emric didn't say anything, he just held me closer and rubbed my back.

"What do we do when we're scared?" He asked me like he used to when we were kids. "We hold on to the things that make us brave, we find courage where there is none, and we find bravery within others and not ourselves, because no one is ever truly alone when they're scared, there is always someone to hold your hand in the dark, your shadow never leaves you even when it's dark." I exclaimed every word and every syllable like dad taught us.

We are never truly alone, and when we're scared we should never fear the unknown but embrace it with all its opportunities. "How are you feeling?" Emric asked again as his hand rubbed my back. "Better, though this position reduces my masculinity." I whined and he scoffed. "You've been by my side our whole lives, how can this be anything other than me being here for you brother." He expressed making me feel calm and happy.

"I guess you're right, I just don't know how to face him, what don't I even say, how do I even say it, it's not like I can just dive in and hope it's not the shallow end of the pool and hopefully get no concussion." I mumbled and Emric hummed. "That is a conundrum, but remember Train, I was once in the same spot you're in, and although our circumstances are different the confession is never different, it's difficult, challenging, and terrifying." He asserted and I was baffled.

"You were afraid when you told Linden about wolves?" I question with unhinged curiosity, Emric was alpha, the bravest person I knew and I never knew him to be scared or frightened, he was sturdy and did not waver, hearing him say he was scared was a shock to me more than anything.

"I was terrified and not because of the confession directly but of losing the man I loved, even before I knew we were mates I knew we belonged together, and if he had rejected me then because the secret was out, I didn't know what I would've done, maybe it would have been different when we turned eighteen and he would be my mate, the bond would've made things easier but it would still be terrifying." My brother explained and sure enough I felt the same way.

I had no idea what I would do if I lost my starfish, he understood me, loved me, and cared about me, he was there when I needed loving the right way, he was perfect for me, and my confession to being a wolf would have it going down the drain and I was terrified.

The prospect of him not wanting me was on the cards, who would want a man with a second animalistic soul within them, not everyone was like Linden and not everyone could be like him, he was just like mom or dad, he understood even without saying a lot, he saw past the fur, would my own mate do that, I wanted so badly for a rogue attack to happen so I would shift and fight for my mate then he wouldn't be scared of me.

I snorted to the thought, if only. "You're thinking too hard, and you're frown line in showing." Emric remarked poking my forehead where my supposed frown line was, it would show whenever I was racking my brain for answers or how to deal with a problem that had no right way of solving.

"I'm thinking about him, I went on a rampage Emric, I let my wolf lose control and did all that—." I couldn't say it even now, I knew what I was doing but my anger and fury clouded everything plus with no control over my wolf it was more so my fault, if I had only stayed inside beside my mate maybe it wouldn't have happened.

"They deserved it Train so don't you dare feel guilty about it, he could've died Train, and they would've acted like it was nothing and probably covered it up so no one would know about it, we got there in time to make sure it didn't happen, but for your wolf, it was blood for blood, I'm sure as hell if my own unwanted mother inlaw had done something to mama munchie I would've rampaged." He asserted proudly speaking of his mate and justifying my actions.

I sighed with slight amusement thinking of Linden's pet name that had slipped from Emric, mama munchie indeed. Though I was having trouble believing what I did was right I wouldn't voice it out as I only needed Andie to tell me it was okay that I did it, and that he wouldn't hate me for it.

I had now two things to worry about, telling him that I was a wolf and the fact that I had ripped his parents apart and left only enough to make sure they didn't die, the ST Maine police department would claim it was a rabid wolf that attacked them that was obvious but if I were to tell my mate then he would know I did it.

No matter how much I fumbled with words I couldn't find the right ones to actually convey how I felt, did I need to start with an apology, or did I dive right in and wait for him to respond with shock and then understanding, my mind was on a tailspin and I didn't know if I could do it.

"What do I say, how do I say it?" I asked Emric and he chuckled deeply as his voice was now deep and yet surprisingly soothing. "Hey stop laughing, I'm serious." I whined punching his eight pack which more or less looked like ten, and he obviously didn't feel it. "Fine, fine I'm sorry." He calmed down laying on the bed with my head on his chest, it was amusing how both of us had fit on it.

"Train, you don't need some perfectly crafted speech to talk to him, you just need to say whatever you feel, a crafted speech is like a meticulous lie, you're not saying the truth you're just saying the words hoping they convey what you want the other person to believe but in hindsight that's not how you truly feel at all." He stated sternly with his all wise eyes looking at me and a smile on his lips.

"Linden is rubbing off you isn't he, Mr wise alpha." I teased and he scoffed with a proud stare. "If he doesn't rub me off who will, he is my mate." He replied with a smirk and I facepalmed making him laugh again. "Not like that!" I yelled as we both burst out laughing, it made me feel better, but Em was right I need to just dive in and hopefully not at the shallow end.

"I'm gonna take that advice to heart." I conceded and he smiled. "I know you will." He mumbled as we lay on the bed, I didn't know how he was going to react but I was prepared to beg him if need be, I couldn't lose him.

+++

I love writing these brother moments a lot, hope you enjoy them too.

Follow - Vote - Comment

LMJ

15.

A love like no other is a love that embraces a person whole, with all their beautiful flaws.Linden O. Everlin.

Andrew.

"I was finally fully awake, my mind wasn't hazy, I knew where I was and all my heart wanted was to have him in my arms, I was slightly going out of my mind with the waiting game but I've been a master at the waiting game, so I waited patiently.

It's funny how I've always waited for so much in my life that I've learned to be patient myself as well, I never dated anyone knowing my one guy would come, I never pursued anything besides art even when I messed it up because I knew my day would come and I would shine, my patience was pretty much spread out.

I chuckled to the thought of having to wait on our wedding day, it made me blush and amuse me. I just needed to know he was okay, to let him know that I was okay and we didn't need to worry anymore, I was free to be with him, love him and never let him go, that's what I hoped for anyway, a fool in love can only dream.

The door opened slowly and there he stood, my heart rate picked up, it was no longer beating steadily, my palms were sweaty and a weird breeze went up my spine, he was irresistibly beautiful and he made my body haywire, my senses go out of sync and my body even more so bent to just anything he said.

He stood there as I looked into his eyes, he did the same with me, no words had been spoken but the tears that stung my eyes were evidence enough I was unbelieving that this was real, he was a disheveled mess but he was mine.

"Starfish." He mumbled. "Seamonster." I replied and within seconds I was wrapped up in his large arms, I felt the block on our mind link disappear and everything he felt hit me like a truck, I held on to him, relishing the feeling of his happiness, of the reassuring hold that he was indeed there.

I cried in his arms because I thought I had lost him, that I would never see him again, never touch him, feel him, breathe in his scent, most of all I was terrified of never getting a chance to love him, it was all that I was afraid of but in his arms, I felt better, I felt reassured and the negativity that had circulated in my thoughts and emotions vanished.

It was replaced by a warm fuzzy feeling, the feeling he had always brought when he held me. "I thought I lost you." He mumbled and I scoffed at the sheer coincidence that we felt the same thing, feared the same thing. "I thought I lost you, my sea monster of the deep." I replied and he squeezed me again in his large arms.

"Is this real?" I mumbled and he nodded. "You're not dreaming starfish, I'm real, you're real, everything is okay my baby."' He reassured and I clung to him for dear life. I cried all over again, but these tears washed away my doubts and insecurities, I knew it was time to have that talk so that the gap between us could be bridged.

I had to do it for him, he had taken my pain and I was going to take away his doubts and fears, it's what mates did for each other, its what I'd do for him, now and always. So as I moved to lay my head on his chest and he laid on the bed I heaved a sigh along with a sniffle and made myself comfortable on his broad chest.

"I know about everything." I mumbled and the shock wasn't all too far away along with panic. "Don't fret it's okay Train, calm down." I tried soothing him as I brushed my hand on his ripped torso. I knew he would have questions but he needed to calm down which as we lay on the bed he did.

"Linden and Emric told me and showed the morning before we went on our road trip, they told me your reason for not telling me, and I kept it to myself because I thought you would tell me, but over time being in here I realized how terrified you must've been so you didn't tell me, I know you fear being left alone and I understand, but sea monster you have to understand that I would never leave you not in this life or the next." I confessed and wordlessly he pressed a kiss to my head.

"Thank you, thank you." He responded and I held onto him till he was calm again. "So you're not going to freak out, panic and faint?" He questioned and I shook my head. "Not on this one lover, I want you, all of you." I stated and he beamed a smile toward me. "I didn't know how to tell you, I'm sorry that I took this long but I'm not as brave as most." He confessed but I really didn't care though.

"Brave or not my love, I don't care, you're all mine and I don't mind if you're not the strongest or smartest, or the most courageous wolf in the pack, that's not why I fell in love with you, I fell in love with you even before you bit me and sealed our fate together." I exclaimed and the bashful smile never left his face. "I love you, Andrew." He mumbled and I knew he loved me with all his heart I could feel it with our bond.

"No more blocking the mind link, no more avoiding questions when things are weird with your eyes, okay." I asserted and he grinned. "I promise my starfish no more." His charming attitude had finally started to show as the tension that lingered between us was dissipating now, I was happy in the moment we were in.

"I have to tell you something." He asserted and I hummed in response. "I went on a rampage, my wolf had control, I was so angry at your parents for what they did and I just couldn't control myself." He stopped to gather himself and I remained silent to hear what he wanted to say.

"It was after your surgery, I needed air so I went outside, your blood was still on my hands and so I shifted so I could clear my mind with a run, but it did no good, I attacked your parents." He confessed. "I'm so sorry starfish, I didn't mean for it to go that far but it did." He added and some part of me was proud for whatever he did.

Karma was well on its way to my parents and what better way to deliver it than an angry beast. "Whatever you did I forgive you and your wolf." I reassured and Train seemed shocked by my response. "But you don't know what we did." He accused. "I don't need to know, my parents were in karma's bitch list for a while so if they got it then I don't care really." I expressed my feelings on the matter.

It wasn't because I was angry but because I wanted my parents to feel what I felt, to know how much they hurt me, aslong as they were not dead and would live with the consequences of their actions I was strangely okay with that. "I guess when you read the headline for today you won't be shocked." He mumbled and I chuckled because of how amused I was by his relief.

I was consumed in my desire for Train, nothing he could do in my eyes would have me stop loving him. "I would like to see your wolf form once I'm out of this place." I stated and he smiled making me blush. "You have no idea how much my wolf would love that." He replied his eyes changing from blue to gold, I could stare into them forever.

I inched closer to him, until our lips met in a breathtaking kiss, suddenly he was on top of me hands roaming my skin, and lips leaving bruises and bites on my neck. "Train uh." I moaned when his large rod ground on mine, he kept grinding eliciting moans from me.

My hospital gown was torn off and his shorts discarded, his hard shaft slapped on my belly making me drool at the length and how wet it was. "See how hard you make me." He teased again as we kissed.

"Fuck I missed this." He grunted whilst his cock and mine were in his palm, he jerked us both and pleasure exploded all over me, he kept stroking us together faster and faster making ripples of pleasure roam my body. "Make me cum please." I begged as both our cocks were wet with the precum oozing from his.

It was large with veins protruding from every part of it pulsing with need, as he stroke again his cock released more precum wetting both our cocks, he grinded with a slight thrust making me moan, his mouth latched on to my nipple sucking and biting making me feel everything intensified.

"Please let me fuck uh—." I was cut off when he pumped both our lengths, I couldn't contain it any longer. "I'm about to cum on you cum starfish, want it?" He teased but incoherent words came from my mouth as he jerked again and seed spewed from my cock, squirting on my stomach and his, his own cum spread all over my stomach and the sheet below, it always amazed me how his load was always big.

"You still got it." I mumbled as he panted beside me. "Wait till I get you out of this hospital, I'm gonna make sure you don't walk for a day." He retorted and somehow I was looking forward to that.

+++

LMJ

16.

Lanks ~ Stronger Than.

Andrew.

"Welcome home, I hope it feels like home." Linden announced as he opened the door to a suite at the mansion where the pack lived, most of the those who lived here according to Linden were the recently mated couples, single warriors, and pack members who preferred living in the mansion than in a house, usually, the option was there but the Luna encouraged living together as a way to strengthen pack spirit.

But if you just didn't like living at the pack house all you needed to do was to request for the house and it got sorted. "I love this place." I had only entered the suite but it was so homey, warm, and perfectly decorated, my art pieces were on the walls along with vases and additional by Linden.

"I knew that would make it better." Linden mumbled next to me and I nodded in acknowledgement, the place was amazing. "I love this thank you Linden and Emric, is that okay if I call you that, Train calls you Em or alpha half the time." I fumbled over my words and he chuckled.

"Em, is fine, but when the situation calls for it you will know to address me as alpha, don't worry you'll get the hang of it." He explained warmly and I nodded feeling peaceful in the place I was. I had never felt like that before, it had indeed baffled me to feel that way, I may have called my previous home my own but I never felt peace.

It was different than where I was, I truly felt like I belonged, with a charming father in law and a mother in law who oozed maternal love, an older brother who made me feel protected and secure, and lastly a friend and brother who I could count on, for almost anything.

I was blessed in a beautiful way and I knew it, I would always be grateful for how my life was turning out, I had no regrets or doubts about the path I was going on. "Andrew dear can I talk to you?" Mrs. Everlin asked as she gestured for me to follow her to what I assumed was a bedroom.

"This is your main bedroom, make yourself at home." I nodded and placed the bag in my hand on the bed, along with flopping myself on the extremely soft bed. I was in heaven on that mattress. "Yeah I know." Mrs. Everlin chortled and I blushed. "It was Linden who bought these beds when he and Emric moved in, I didn't know how much comfort memory foam had until Linden got it for us." She explained and we both chuckled.

"So you wanted to talk about something?" I asked after we had gathered ourselves. "Don't worry it's nothing bad, I just wanted to talk about school, I know your parents weren't in support of you pursuing Art as a major, but honey that's your dream and your passion, I'm hundred percent in support of it, Lex and I love your artwork and we want you to continue with it and thrive." Her words stunned me into silence.

My parents had never taken an interest in my art, they had never taken an interest in anything I wanted, having Mrs. Everlin someone who was like a parent to me acknowledge me for my art was heartwarming, I felt loved and appreciated, so I moved from where I sat and hugged her.

"Thank you." I mumbled and she held me tightly. "I'm here for these hugs sweetheart you can always count on me to be there, any of us, we will be there for you." She reassured wiping away my tears. "Now you've been offered a scholarship to cover half the basics but not everything, that's why you've been working at the boutique right?" I nodded.

The scholarship covered half the cost but what it covered wasn't the essentials needed, and I was trying to have enough money to cover the other half. "This isn't pity, remember that, but Lex and I support our kids to the best of our abilities and you're part of the family, and also our child in a way, so we're going to pay for everything, scraping away that scholarship and letting you enjoy learning art, living with your mate." She stated with a smile and I gasped.

"What?" I croaked. "You heard me kiddo." She teased and I embraced her again. "It's so much money, I can't pay it back." I argued but she chuckled. "I didn't say we want to be paid back, we're doing this as parents not because we want something in return." She mused and I held back a sob, this was kindness I never knew.

"And by the way, a quarter of St Maine businesses are under the Everlin name, money is not an issue, so when you go to college, I want you to live your best college life." She exclaimed with a smile and I reciprocated that loving smile, I knew she wouldn't take back her offer and her smile or eyes did not hold pity, she was indeed doing this out of love.

"Thank you so much." I exclaimed as yet again I hugged her. "You're welcome darling, get settled in, join me and Linden in the kitchen, I'm sure you don't want to miss his cooking." I shook my head and she shooed me away. I walked into the closet as the door closed behind me.

I picked out my clothes and lay them by a small table in the closet, and made it through another door to the bathroom making me realize it was adjoined. I already loved my new home. I stripped to shower and clean away the slight scent of lemon and detergent on me, I had spent the week on a hospital bed since the day Train and I talked.

"You look beautiful." I knew who the voice belonged to and I made space for him in the shower. "I always look beautiful to you." I retorted and he nodded. "Which is true, you're breathtaking, mesmerizing, and most of all intoxicating." Each word was accentuated with a kiss on my shoulder.

"Sea monster we'll play later, right now we need to get to the kitchen because Linden is there working his magic." I tried convincing him and at first, it hadn't worked but the mention of Linden and food had him cleaning me instead of groping me and abusing my senses. "Yeah I know the love of food is real." I mused as we got through the shower in more or less record time.

I picked out his clothes, which felt like the right thing to do, and handed them to him. "So I'm going to be with you, twenty four of seven." He chortled pulling me into his embrace. "Yes my devilish sea monster." I purred and he seemed happy and content to hold me as I was to be held. "I'm in love with you starfish." He asserted nuzzling my hair, a habit which I found strangely odd but liked.

"And I'm in love with you sea monster." I mumbled as my hands tugged on his hair and his chest had a low rumble, I found that he liked it when I played with his hair or just merely scratched his head. "I think I smell hidden egg muffins." He mumbled and I knew Linden had put them out fresh from the oven.

Train tossed me over his shoulder and ran to the kitchen. "I knew you two would be here first." Linden chortled and both my mate and I tried to hide our embarrassment. "Mama munchie your Papi is hungry." Emric came beside us and as expected his muffins and his juice were handed to him. "Love you, Papi." Linden pressed a kiss to his giant mate who walked away.

"Four hour cycles?" Mrs. Everlin questioned. "Of course." Linden replied and the two burst out laughing. "Peanut here you go, put starfish down." Linden ordered and I was put down whilst my mate took his food and walked to his brother. "Wait, peanut?" I asked and Linden nodded.

"How is a freaking huge wolf called peanut." I exclaimed and Linden laughed. "Same way one is called munchie, now eat your food child." He replied and I chuckled taking my food, I truly felt at peace in a new home with people who would do anything for me.

+++

Follow - Vote - Comment

LMJ

17.

Train.

"Now that you're well rested, your mate is absolutely fine and back in school, already planning to have a blaze of glory with his paintings again, will you help me fix this whole mess with Davey." Emric recited the good things in my life as I found myself in his office after school, I envied the fact that he graduated early, now I was suffering alone.

"Fine, I'm here to help and what is it that you require of me alpha?" I asked and he sighed. I knew the same old story of Davey being the cause of problems was now getting to him, with the pack doctor having given Linden an actual due date to pop, his nerves were everywhere and he did not need the stress.

"Calm down Emric I'm sure we just need to meet Tai, take him to the Ordell house, get Mrs. Ordell and Dean there as well and let Davey confess his heartfelt feelings so we can get rid of him." I stated and he seemed amused for some reason which I found none but he still was. "What's so funny?" I asked and he sighed.

"I'm literally kicking out my brother in law from the pack, it just amusing how the person I'm supposed to like and have mutual respect for is a total asshole and the opposite of it all." He exclaimed with a chuckle and I did find what he said was amusing, we were taught to value family but what if the family screwed up so many times you just had to say enough is enough and throw them out.

"It has to be done, whether you like it or you don't plus on the bright side you get see your mother in law." The alpha gave me a flat look then quirked an eyebrow, his message was clearly really and I chuckled making him roll his eyes. "You know how I feel about that woman, I hate her and somehow understand her which makes me hate her even more." It was true Mrs. Ordell and Linden's relationship always had you hating her then confuse you a little then you realize you absolutely hate her.

"I get you brother but there is nothing you can do, speaking of which, does she know you're engaged to her son?" I chortled and he scoffed. "And who would find time in their day to tell her that when her own son can't even stand the sight of her?" The alpha retorted and I sighed, Mrs Ordell was forever hated by my brother and his mate, hopefully their kids will like their grandmother.

Well hopefully, but I'm sure they will be fine with or without them, with uncles like me and Andie who wouldn't be awesome. "So shall we go now or we wait till you stop texting my best friend." I questioned and he raised his finger to cut me off, he was talking to his mate, I decided to talk to mine.

Who decided to send me a pretty sexy picture which kind of got me horny and half hard, yeah I needed to cool off, anything starfish did just seemed sexy and always had me hardening. I needed to cool off, so I texted an I love you to him and turned back to Em who was grinning like a fool.

"You coming over for dinner tonight, it's game night plus Linden is making his secret recipe alfredo and pot roast, for some reason he's in the mood for meat." Emric exclaimed with a grin and I sighed. "You do know he's hinting at the other meat, right." I pointed out and my brother smirked. "Oh no he means meat in actuality, if he wants my raw meat he doesn't have code he just states it like it is, which he did of course." Emric said proudly and my jaw hit the floor.

"Damn, okay two kids wasn't enough you're planning to have more before the first two even pop out." I accused and Emric chuckled. "Relax sergeant overprotective, we'll separate our kids by two years, which is my plan, Marquee has five so I wanna beat that record." The alpha stated proudly even his wolf was showing with pride, my poor Linden I could only hope for his body to be ready to work overtime.

"Okay as shocking as this information is, we might want to get a move on, Tai will make a move sooner or later." I remarked and Emric banged his head on the table. "Do we really have to do this, Linden is showing me the good stuff for the babies, if I don't listen he'll have my balls." Emric whined and I burst out laughing.

"If he threatens your balls then there would be a reason for it, just multi task, and ask questions a lot, if you don't he'll know, I've been there." I expressed and he grinned. Whenever Linden is talking whether it's through the link, phone, or in person always pay attention, if you don't, you don't get the good stuff, I didn't get pancakes with blueberries and cream for two weeks just because I didn't listen to him.

"Nice tip." He mumbled as we made it out of his office, we waved at the pack members who were back from patrol and some from their jobs. The pack was thriving as it always did, with the expansion of St Maine into a city, more wolves had turned up, a background check and you went from rogue to a beloved pack member.

Though some rogues still preferred life on their own terms if hunters were to come they would die, but we've had little to no casualties with rogues ever since we moved here, except Mrs. Ordell's kidnapping, which honestly was boring as fuck, they didn't put a fight.

After driving whilst Emric texted his one and only mama munchie we arrived at the diner I first met Tai Colden. "What are we doing here?" The alpha asked and I rolled down the windows, he sniffed the air and a growl escaped his lips. "He had the audacity to claim this diner as a hang out, it's my favorite in this whole city." He growled and I held my breath, never get in the way of an angry 6'9 alpha.

"Come on." He ordered after texting Linden of course and we walked into the diner. I spotted Tai immediately who was among a group of wolves. "Hello Mr. Everlin, special order as always?" The manager of the diner asked when he saw Emric who smiled and nodded to the man. "Make it four orders." He corrected and turned to Tai.

"So you're the little bitch alpha in my city." Emric addressed Tai who growled in his response and I felt sorry for him. "Here you go Mr. Everlin, I put it on your tab." The manager held out the orders and I took them with a smile. "Alpha I will take these to the car." I mumbled and scurried away to the car, food always had to be saved.

As I closed the door to my car, several bodies ran out and some humans aswell, Tai was flung from his seat through the window and landed just in front of my car. I really should've told him to shove his pride aside and not challenge an alpha way stronger than him. "Get in whatever crappy car you have, we're going to your mates house." Emric ordered and Tai scrambled to get to a jeep that was parked at the end of the bay, Emric got in as well.

I knew I was to follow them, and so I followed. "Fire on fire would normally kill us But this much desire, together we're winners They say that we're out of control and some say   we're sinners But don't let them ruin our beautiful rhythms " I sang as I followed behind the jeep.

As we got to the Ordell house I had practically repeated the song three times. "Move." Emric instructed as he got out of the jeep, I climbed out of my car and followed the two inside. "What's going on Emric?" It was Mrs. Ordell who had answered the door shocked to see us there.

"Evening alpha." Dean mumbled as we followed his mate inside, the two looked relatively good, but I didn't focus on them as Davey walked downstairs, he gasped looking at Tai and Emric and I smirked. He was totally busted.

+++

I just loved writing this chapter, it was lively fun and everything just flowed for me, I'm a fan of brother moments and these ones with Train and Emric are always fun.

Fire on Fire by Sam Smith is actually the theme song for this book, well one of them anyway, am I still talking, shit, oh well.

Vote - Comment - Follow - Share

LMJ

18.

Train.

"Hello love." Tai exclaimed looking at Davey, it seemed the man couldn't find a persona to weasel into therefore just stood there frozen like a fish stick, it's these moments in my life I wish I had popcorn at the ready, too much shit had to come out and Davey literally had to come clean.

"Wolf got your tongue, Davey?" I snickered and Emric scoffed. "Tai, what are you doing here?" It seemed Mrs. Ordell was confused and shocked to know that her son knew the man who had been brought to her house. "What the hell is going on Davey?" Dean growled and I chuckled lightly, this was not going well for Davey.

"Before you act like you know nothing, don't, before you even attempt to lie, don't, if you do I will make lover boy's pelt here a rug for my kids to play with." Emric growled and I was smugly proud standing behind him, that was my alpha right there. "I said what the hell is going on, by the goddess start talking Davey!" Dean yelled and I turned to face him again surprised he had the balls to be in charge like that.

"Its nothing, I just know him that's all." The man exclaimed and both Em and I scoffed, knowing him was putting it lightly or rather, knowing him meant all of him, I would never know. "Stop pretending mon cheri, they know about us and I suspect the alpha's brother does as well." Tai confessed and Davey's facade crumbled.

He immediately ran to Tai and wrapped his arms around his torso. "Did they hurt you?" Davey mumbled checking Tai for any injuries. "Nothing that won't heal, but I'm afraid the plan failed." Tai replied and I wondered what plan was this exactly. "Are you and this man together Davey?" Mrs. Ordell finally questioned, her shock had worn off so the questions were now coming.

"Yes mom, this is Tai, Tai my mother." Davey introduced and Emric growled. "I didn't come here so you could introduce one of your men to your mother, I want you to tell her what you and this particular wolf planned together, after doing so your mother will know why I'm letting the man you love take you away rather than I kill him." The alpha explained and it seemed Davey was baffled into silence yet again.

My theory on what they had done together was now coming true, they had indeed planned everything together. "Well we're waiting." I urged and Davey glared at me before turning to his mother. "What did you do Davey Ordell say it now!" Mrs. Ordell screamed and her mate calmed her down.

"Mom I think it's best you sit down." He replied. "It's quite the long love story." Tai added and Emric punched him making him double over in pain and it also made him silent. The only woman in the room and her mate moved to the couch. "Mom I did some bad stuff while I was away which I never told you—."

He began to narrate what happened since he left, the day he met the rogue alpha Tai, and how they fell in love, how he never judged him even though he was a wolf, they didn't expect Davey to have a mate who was a wolf since he was a human but it got complicated when J. Turner appeared in their lives.

The bond made feelings for Turner bud in Davey but he was human and could never fully grasp the concept of a mate, so even though Turner loved him, Davey never loved Turner like he thought he would, so after a failed relationship he went back to the rogue who offered him a deal for his love.

Davey couldn't go through with the deal so he came up with another plan, he told the plan to Tai and left Turner to find the note that broke his heart, he knew Turner as a wolf would follow him anywhere but Turner grew bitter and hated Davey for leaving him, there he tracked down Davey and rejected him.

With Turner out of the picture it was now easy for Davey to get back to Tai, it was a really thought out plan but that wasn't the highlight of it, Tai expected Davey to find a way into the Ryeland pack, over time after the two had settled well in the pack Tai would challenge the alpha, if he were to win then the Ryeland pack would have a new alpha.

Their plan was insulting and idiotic, I suppose it had to be that way because Davey didn't expect his little brother to be mated to the alpha, he didn't expect the alpha to be stronger than the one he was to help take over the Ryeland, they had overestimated their win and now they were paying for it.

Mrs. Ordell was in one word shocked, she sat silently listening to everything Davey had said, it didn't take a shrink to know that she wanted to beat the shit out of her son for doing what he did. "Alpha, what is your judgment?" Dean asked avoiding to look at Tai or Davey, there was nothing they could do anyway.

"I let you live in my pack territory, I gave you protection and this is how you repay me, I should've banished your mother and her mate but instead

I let her stay here with her mate protected by my pack, and you bring this to my pack." Emric growled looking at Davey.

"I warned you before, it seemed you didn't listen, pack your things and leave St Maine, I don't care where you go just leave, as for you Mrs. Ordell, choose, either live here or follow your son out, you have twelve hours to decide." Emric concluded and Mrs. Ordell along with her mate nodded, Davey remained silent and Tai was blank.

"And Tai don't ever step foot in that diner or my city." The alpha warned Tai and I followed behind him silently. As we got to the car Emric sat on the passenger side and I turned the ignition, before I could drive away the mind link with my mate opened.

"Babe come to the street where I used to live now, but lay low." He instructed and I sped off toward my mates old street. "Train that's the long way home." Emric reprimanded but I pointed in front of us where Andie was talking to a man I didn't know, I already knew he was a wolf though.

"I'm looking for my son, here is his picture, I asked the lady by that house and she told me to speak to you, I don't know why." I could hear him through Andie's thoughts and I could tell he's lying. "Babe he has a photo of you." Andie relayed and I gripped the steering tighter. "It can't be him, can it." I mumbled feeling my anger spike.

"Tell me that man did not just claim to be your bio father." Emric growled and I nodded. "Can I kill him now and get it over with?" He added and I suppressed the urge to kill him myself. We couldn't risk exposing ourselves and we didn't have all the information, so it was best to just lay low.

"I'm sorry I haven't seen him in a while, he used to live a couple of houses from mine but it's like he vanished, and it's been a while, I'm so sorry but I can keep an eye out for you, give me your number, oh yeah where are you staying so I can easily find you." Starfish relayed their conversation to me yet again through the link, the man gave my baby a card, they parted ways after.

Andie kept moving and walked past us, he winked at Emric and kept walking down the street till it bent and he was out of sight. "The man is gone, move we need to pick up your mate." He ordered and I wondered what was going on.

We finally caught up with Andie and he hopped into the car with a grin plastered on his face. "Good job." Emric commented as my starfish handed over the card and his phone to Emric. "What's going on?" I questioned and the two chuckled.

"We couldn't obviously confront the guy, so I had your amazing mate ask him for his phone number and address so a squad can track him and my amazing mate can hack into his phone." Emric proudly stated and he fist bumped with Andie.

"Hey baby, we're going to figure out everything okay, but for now let's go heat these up and eat, whilst I beat your ass at Mario Kart." I sighed knowing my starfish was right, we could take care of this easily but the thought of having a man parading around with a picture of me claiming to be my father was unsettling.

My father was Lex Everlin and he has been the best father I could ever ask for, I didn't need a sperm donor claiming me as his own, so I shoved the thoughts aside and focused on game night. "You're on lover."

+++

LMJ

19.

Train.

"Okay, his name is Fred Lloyd, he lives in Algiers, he's a rogue, but living in the city he's more civilized than most, you can barely tell he's a rogue unless he's got a pack he belongs to any way he came here a month ago." My best friend explains the information he's getting off the man's phone who was supposedly my father.

"I didn't know you could hack into phones or laptops" Andie pipes in and Linden chuckled. "I have a lot of free time now, I learned how to do it in one day." Linden smugly replied but I wasn't surprised, he was impressive. "Back to the matter at hand, mama munchie do you have anything else?" Emric asked his mate with a smile.

"Oh yeah, he has a birth record probably Train's, and there is a DNA report in one of his documents, but you need some sort of DNA from the person you want to run it against, like hair, nails or saliva how could he have gotten that and used it to have that report." Linden argued baffling me, it seemed Fred had been busy the month he had been here.

"Is it possible he followed him around and somehow was able to get his DNA, like at school, there, it would have been easy or his car." Andie suggested and all his claims held water, had this man followed me in pursuit to prove I was his son. I knew I had to confront him that was the only way.

"The only way to know for certain is if you confront him, that's the best way to solve all this, and he needs to go back to wherever he came from, he's not wanted here." Linden voiced out and those were my thoughts as well, I didn't want to know a man who knew I existed for eighteen years to finally show up now when I was finally an independent adult.

I would've welcomed the idea when I was a naive four year old but not now, he had to leave and I had to make sure of it, mom and dad didn't need the worry of me going with him or sitting at a round table entertaining him, I couldn't do that to my parents, therefore this man had to go before they knew.

"You're right Linden, I will meet up with him, and tell him to leave, I can't do this now when I've accepted who I am, completely happy with the parents that wanted me." I reassured my own conviction in those words and my starfish hugged me, I breathed in his scent and it calmed me down.

"Let me text him." I explained and Andie handed me my phone. I texted Fred and told him to meet me by the diner on the west end, I was hoping it was refurbished by now, they had a lovely patio, and the sun would be just right. "I'm coming with you." Andie asserted but I shook my head.

"But babe." He argued but this was best. "I need to do this on my own, I need to confront him myself and if anything goes in any way wrong you'll be okay." I argued and he nodded in understanding. "I know you want to be there for me, but you already are, you're my mate and I always have a piece of you wherever I go." I added placing a kiss on his forehead.

"I love you." I whispered. "I love you too." He mumbled in response. "Be careful peanut, and remember don't give in to any crap okay." Linden instructed and I nodded whilst placing a kiss in his hair. "Link is open!" I yelled as I got out of Linden and Emric's house.

I drove to the diner and found it newly refurbished even after Emric threw a wolf out the front window, it seemed to being rich and an alpha always had its perks. I spotted Fred by the patio enjoying the sun and sipping juice.

I scoffed looking at the man, for some reason he claimed to be my father but I looked nothing like him, Lex Everlin wasn't my father but I had pretty much inherited his looks, which I'm proud to say that I'm hot.

After texting Emric and turning on my phone location so Linden knew where I was, I got out of the car and headed for the man, the closer I got the more I saw the resemblance between our eyes. "You're here." He mumbled standing up and I quirked a brow. Had he not expected me to show up when I was the one who approached him first.

"I heard you're looking for me." I stated not caring for formalities. "Uh, yes I have, it's nice to meet you, after all this time, you've become a fine young man." He expressed as my anger flickered. "And you expect me to know you how and why?" I questioned and he seemed baffled by my response.

"I know it's a lot that I'm about to say but please keep an open mind." He urged and I nodded. "I'm your biological father, the man you've lived with all your life, Lex and his wife are not your parents, I'm your parent, your mother died during childbirth." It wasn't the blatant lie that baffled me, it was the audacity to even try.

"You're not a good liar Mr. Lloyd, the alpha you casually spoke of is my father and his wife is my mother, I know I'm not their biological son because they told me the truth, showed me the hospital footage of what happened that night, my mother didn't die during childbirth, she gave me away, and you were never around." I argued and his face paled.

"I tried looking for you, in North City, Algiers, SandBury but I could never find you." His statement made me look back at a question I wanted him to answer. "How long have you known about me being alive, and did you know where my mother was?" I questioned and the question seemed to take him off guard.

"I knew ever since you were born, I'm a wolf so I knew, I was a rogue and a coward son, I couldn't take care of you and your mother so I ran." His response made my wolf angry. "So you left us, and she in turn abandoned me, all this while you knew I was alive, you knew about my parents therefore you knew where I was." I asserted and any sort of denial left his eyes.

"I wanted to take you with me, but you had found a good home, one I couldn't provide son." He tried to defend himself, which made me angry. "Stop calling me son!" I punched him as he sat on the chair opposite me. "You had the chance to be a father, my whole eighteen years of life, now you come trying to weasel your way into my life when I've become independent, not gonna happen." I spat out sitting down.

He wiped the blood away from his nose and mouth and looked at me. "Understand that I made bad choices I'm just trying to rectify them, give me a chance to be part of your life please." He pleaded and I scoffed. "Answer my second question." I probed and he froze.

"She's back home in Algiers, she wanted to come meet you but your siblings had no one to babysit." His answer made every emotion I felt just drain away, I was their unwanted child, after she gave me up they got back together and forgot they had me, and on top of that, had more kids, I was hurt, betrayed even.

"I want nothing to do with you or your family, you're not my father you're just a sperm donor and your wife was just a surrogate for my parents, don't come near me or my family, don't ask around about me claiming I'm your son, because I am not, if you don't heed my warning I swear I will rip your throat out with my fangs and hang your head on a spike as an example for people who want to meddle in my life." I growled before standing and heading to my car.

I didn't want anything else, I felt hollow and betrayed, I just wanted to go home, so I drove straight to the people who always felt like home.

+++

LMJ

20.

Home is where your heart is but sometimes it's not always your heart, it where the people that fill your heart with love are.Lex Everlin.

Billie Martin ~ Bird.

Train.

It was late afternoon when I parked my car in the driveway to my parents house, I didn't find time to lock the car, I just ran in and didn't care what else. "Mom!" I cried out and she came walking down the stairs her ever warm smile present. "Mom." I choked on my tears.

"Oh, sweetheart." She opened her arms for me and like a child, I clung to her with tears trailing down my cheeks, I couldn't contain it, I felt so betrayed, unwanted, so I let out all that I was feeling. "It was horrible mom, they abandoned me." I cried out and she held me.

"It hurts so much mom, it hurts, mom make it stop hurting." I cried out and she only held me tighter. " It's alright baby mommy's got you, I will take the pain away I'm right here don't you worry, I'm right here." I kept crying as she soothed me, and I clung to her for dear life.

A pair of strong arms engulfed us both and I knew that scent ever since I was a pup. "Dad." I choked on my tears as both my parents held me in their embrace, dad it hurts so much, it's hur—." I broke down all over again. "I'm here champ let it out." I didn't need to hide my feelings or tears from them, I didn't need to be strong or brave, they didn't raise me like that, they loved me and taught me to be a better man.

In their arms I cried, cried for all the pain meeting Fred had caused, years of feeling abandoned came back, the pain of knowing my parents didn't want me and knew I was there but never came once not even just to see me and let me know they loved me, none of it, and it hurt so badly.

I didn't know how to move on from something like this, I only knew my parents would make it better, they were my constant, they held my hand when I fell, embraced my flaws, and accepted me for who I was, I wasn't born to them but at times I wish I had been so that I didn't have to go through all the pain that I do now, I hated the pain.

"Mom I—." I choked again feeling my tears come again and I broke down, she didn't care if I got her dirty she just held me, I could feel dad's tears on my neck as he too held me, when I cried he hurt as well, he was the best father I could ever have, he celebrated with me, enjoyed my moments with me and cried with me when I was sad and never failed to show me he loved me.

So I clung to them, I clung to my home and the parents that loved me before I even loved myself. As I finally calmed down, dad picked me up in his arms and we made it upstairs to my old room and he laid me on the bed right next to him, I fell asleep as he soothed my aching heart with a lullaby.

Today had been nerve wrecking for me, and all I wanted was to feel peace again, to feel better, to let go of the pain I felt, and to just have no inner turmoil, no headaches because I no longer had tears to cry.

When I woke up dad was gone but his scent still lingered on the bed and on my clothes, I turned to look at the shirt I was wearing and the pants, probably one of my parents changed me from what I was wearing. I smiled at the thought, my head no longer throbbed and my heart no longer felt as if it was constricting, I felt better taking in the scent of heavy male musk and the scent of fresh rain and daisies, it was weird how dad smelled like daisies.

It was always weird even now, I made my way downstairs where there was chatter in the kitchen, my mate and my brothers were there, along with our parents. "Hey peanut." Linden waddled to me and I hugged him taking in his scent, it was always calming, I bent down to his stomach and kissed it. "Oh they're kicking." He held on to me and I placed my hand on his stomach.

"Hey guys I'm your uncle." I mumbled and another kick, damn these kids were definitely alphas they kicked a lot. "Damn that's my ribcage." Linden cried out and I chuckled as mom came over and soothed her pregnant son in law. "Oh my, this is how Emric was too, he was a mean kicker, used my bladder as cushion to bounce on." She chortled rubbing Linden's back.

"I'm close to popping any day now I can literally feel it." He mumbled the response to mom and she nodded too. Emric winked at me and went back to playing his game, I knew it was the we will talk later wink and I moved to my mate. "I'm sorry." He mumbled and I led him to the library.

"I'm so sorry." I held him as he cried in my arms, I knew he held felt what I felt, and heard some of the things Fred had said, it was hurtful I knew, so I let him cry it out. "We're okay starfish, we're okay." I reassured as I held him close. "Parents are just whackjobs huh." He chortled. "Not all of them." I replied with a chuckle. "True, not all of them." He conceded as nothing more was said between us only our kisses conveyed it all.

"I love you." He whispered. "And I'm in love with you Andrew Krest." I responded and he smiled to it. "I think I wanna be an Everlin now, my surname is a little too depressing." He corrected and I placed a kiss on his forehead. "That can easily be arranged." I replied kissing him again.

"Let's have dinner, your mom made curry." He announced after we parted our lips and we made our back to the lounge where Emric was talking to his kids and Linden was talking to my father. "Those three are in a world of their own, you might as well help me set the table." Mom asserted and we got to work helping my mom with the dinner table.

"You feeling better sweetheart?" Mom asked with a smile and I nodded enthusiastically. "Good, never forget what your father says, home is where the people who fill your heart—." I cut her off. "Who fill your heart with love are." I finished for her and she smiled. "Exactly, I'm always here for you, all of you." She added placing a kiss on my forehead.

"Lex darling dinner, Linden is probably starving!" Mom called out and Emric carried his mate to the dinner table, on one end dad sat and the other Emric, mom took the right seat by dad and so did Linden, I sat next to the pregnant man and Andie next to my mother. "This is so good." I exclaimed shoving more curry down my throat.

"Whoa babe slow down, its all yours." Starfish reprimanded and my cheeks turned red with embarrassment, but who could blame me I was a wolf, a very hungry wolf, and my mother makes some good curry like seriously good curry.

"Have you thought of baby names yet?" I asked Linden and he shook his head. "Haven't had time, we've been busy dealing with Davey, Tai, and Fred, along with Turner, it's been a full plate lately and really hard to keep up but hopefully we will come up with something." Emric replied as he fed Linden.

"Okay, I have suggestions but I will air them in two days." My mate spoke up and I remembered he has a surprise baby shower for Linden, I get to see my favorite alpha and his mate, as chatter at the table went on, I realized that I was happy right where I was, my decision to make sure Fred wasn't part of my life had been the right one for me and I was happy with that, I had everything I wanted.

+++

I was listening to Billie Eilish - Everything I wanted and Billie Martin - Bird, when I wrote this chapter, and the songs just evoked a lot of emotion from me and I hope you felt it too.

Vote - Share - Comment - Follow

LMJ

21.

The Heathens visit.

Train.

"Have you got the baby bottles, if so please fill them with anything alcoholic." My mate ordered, dad and I groaned, we were tired, restless and most of all hungry, my mate had woken us up to help him with the baby shower for Linden, according to him this is one he's to be included therefore he wanted it to be spectacular.

"Get those boxes in the corner please and thank you." He ordered some of the wolves who volunteered to help since their luna was amazing and they wanted to do something special for him, wolves would find any reason to celebrate, eat and fuck, it's just how we are and in this pack, we did that a lot.

"Hey is anyone helping Mrs. Everlin with the food?" He questioned going past us with his head stuck on the checklist in his hand. "I got it!" I yelled and didn't wait for a response. "Train you better sneak me some chow." Dad whispered and I winked at him before running to the kitchen.

"Mom I'm hungry, he's like a drill sergeant today." I whined, even the sex was put on time and schedule, who has sex in two hours ad feels satisfied with that, I needed more to sedate my sea monster but alas my mate put us on a schedule.

"He just wants the day to be perfect for Linden, so you have to forgive him if he's a little extra today, you do remember how I was like on your birthday." She reminded and how could I forget, she made us shop for things till dad and I were beyond exhausted, like we had come from some war, and the highlight of that day was the ten layer cake, goddess it was good.

"How can I ever." I mumbled and she chuckled. "Exactly so let him have his fun, Linden goes easy on you because you're his favorite but not this time, he's not here to save your ass this time." She chortled as I helped her put the bird in the over after marinating it. "Hey mom, dad and I are still hungry, can you sneak us some chow." I pleaded with my puppy dog eyes and she caved.

"Here but remember I know nothing of this, so better swallow not chew." She warned and I burst out laughing. "Mom that's sound wrong, just like the time you mentioned chains." I accused and she rolled her eyes. "Get out of here you dirty minded child." She shooed me away. "By the way we use silk now, the ropes stung, or Egyptian cotton that breathes, the best." I was horrified as she exclaimed her sexcapades with dad.

"Mom stop, I don't want that in my head." She burst out laughing. "You started it sweetheart plus I'm giving you pointers for after all this." She gestured to the numerous things starfish had made us do. "Mom!" I groaned loudly walking away leaving my mother clutching her stomach.

Sometimes I wondered if we were mother and son, we acted like best friends, but I always knew to respect her, even if she didn't give birth to me, the milk that nurtured me was hers I was her son. I gestured for dad to sneak away and follow me, we got to the library and I handed him his food.

"Mom said swallow don't chew." He smirked proudly. "Ah, the old motto, she used to say that whilst we used the ropes, good times." Somehow in all that I cringed, facepalmed, and felt a bit more hungry so instead of paying attention to the other parent with a loose mouth, I got down to eat my food, my perverted parents came second to food.

After obviously swallowing like a pro, dad and I made our way back to the lounge that was decorated beautifully, the good stuff had been put in the baby feeders and if you wanted the more good stuff you would have to come directly to me and I got you some.

"Where had you two gone?" My mate inquired and I froze, dad whistled and walked away, he always got a pass somehow and I was the one left to deal with my mate who was about to have me by my balls. "Starfish baby, we was just uh—." I was cut off by the smell of heavy male musk and roses, along with spice and butterscotch, I knew those scents anywhere.

"We're here!" Aries yelled and both my mate and I turned to face him. "Heathen, Aries!" I yelled dragging my mate with me to meet them. "Train, oh my goddess you've grown!" Aries exclaimed excitedly squashing me in his arms.

"Hey favorite alpha." I bro higher Heathen since I couldn't hug him all the way he had baby Savage in his sling. "This is my mate Andrew, Andrew this is Alpha Heathen and his mate Aries, and their baby boy Savage." I introduced my mate to the mountain of a man along with his mate.

"He's so perfect, you are one lucky guy." Aries compliments whilst hugging Andrew, I wasn't bothered with the fact that Heathen was seven feet tall, Emric was mere inches from him so we were okay. He was the strongest alpha in the world though, that was the scary part, but he was a big teddy bear to anyone who knew him.

"You guys made it!" My mother cheered hugging both Heathen and Aries, my father came to them and hugged Aries along with shaking hands with the alpha. "We couldn't miss it for anything." Aries replied with a smile. "The party is here!" Emma yelled walking in with bottles.

"Let's crank this bitch up!" She yelled again and we burst out laughing. "Alvie you came!" She squealed launching herself on her brother. "Of course I did." He replied smugly. "Uncle Heathen!" Raziq launched himself onto the giant man as well luckily my father had taken Savage and the baby was giggling all the way.

"Arent you forgetting someone." Aries teased and Terric rained kisses on Aries along with Raziq. "Okay okay I missed you too!" Aries yelled as they finally released him from their attacks. "So where is my favorite luna?" Heathen asked. "On his way, everybody hide!" Starfish screamed and we all scrambled to hide.

"I swear to the goddess if Andie called me here for kumbaya circle time I will castrate him, does he know how hard it is to move when you have two wolves kicking your ribs like a football!" Linden yelled. "Oh been there." Aries asserted and we all burst out laughing. "What in the —."

"Surprise!" We all yelled and Linden held onto his stomach for dear life. "Goodness gracious you guys, do you want to scare the water break out of me." He exclaimed making all of us. "Oh goddess, you did this, you sneaky bitch!" Linden yelled as he hugged Andrew. "Thank you." He added looking around.

"There's my favorite Luna!" Heathen cheered and Linden's jaws dropped but he was about to burst into a million rainbows. "Heathen!" The pregnant man screamed in glee as he wrapped his arms around the tall mountain of a man. "I missed you." The two stay in the hug a moment longer before Aries takes him.

"Look at you all big and ready to pop." Aries commented as everyone began to chat amongst themselves. "You came, thank you." Linden expressed as he held on to Aries. "Linden, you doing them squats?" Emma quizzed and I chuckled to myself, Emma and Linden always exercise together so that Linden could be okay during birth and after.

"Yes!" He replied and Emma turned to Raziq. "Baby crank this bitch up!" If anyone knew how to party it was Emma or rather the Ryeland pack. Food and drinks were served, people danced and enjoyed the music. "Hey kiddo, Linden told me what happened, you okay?" I smiled toward Heathen and nodded. "Yeah, I had some pretty great support, and I made it through plus I saw your message, I'm great." The alpha hugged me like an older brother.

"Glad to hear to it, anyway give me the good stuff." He mumbled and I slipped him the bottle brewed for wolves, he winked at me and walked to where Emric was. "Emma!" Emric called out and the three slipped away unnoticed, they were really going to get unhinged.

"Thank you, I know you helped." It was Linden who had spoken beside me and I hugged him. "You're welcome, brother." I replied as we got to the couch. Andie was with Raziq laughing at some odd joke and I was glad the two got along. Aries came to join us with Savage in his arms. "Oh he's beautiful as always." Linden exclaimed and it was true the baby was gorgeous.

"Thank you, but I'm not the only one about to make beautiful kids just wait and see." He chortled making all of us laugh. The baby shower which was more of a party had just begun but I knew like Emma had said, we were going to crank this bitch up.

+++

This chapter is dedicated to:@Kickz1080@_Jarvis_18_@valeriefinney41

Thank you for reading my works and loving them, and obviously Heathen, so if you're wondering where Alpha Heathen and his mate Aries come from read my book Heathen.

To This was kinda lowkey dedication to you love.

Follow - Vote - Share

LMJ

22.

Andrew.

I groaned on the bed not wanting to wake up, I was tired, my back was sore, Train was no joke when he wanted to pound you and have you take it without complaints, last night I was shown whose boss. Now I'm feeling the side effects of good sex plus the party that happened a few days ago.

I wanted my hangover to be gone but now I know that a hangover from wolf alcohol will literally kill you, never again, I don't regret the rest of the party, I got to meet amazing people, I got to make amazing new friends, and have people to help me when I needed it.

I groaned yet again when I didn't feel Train next to me, lately I was used to waking up with him by my side now with him obviously going on patrol and training the pack, I missed him, which was sad, I no longer had school, I decided not to go since graduation was tomorrow.

I was going to spend my day pampering myself in the luxurious suite that was my home, I could never really grasp the fact that I was the one who lived in the suite, it was somewhat like a dream and I would wake up with a bang and realize I'm still on my springy double bed, that would be horrible.

I breathed in my mates scent happily, I could never get enough of that smell, it was addictive and intoxicating. "Wake up Andie and do something with yourself." I mumbled before rolling out of bed, I walked to the window and peered outside, the sun was warm, the kids played by the grounds and the teens were going through their morning drill.

The pack warrior were fighting like gladiators as always with sweat glistening over rock hard abs, sculptured V-lines, and tempting packages, I chuckled to myself as some of the teens were checking out every gay boy's dream, sweaty, sexy, half naked men training, only thing that was missing, was popcorn.

I looked around till I found my own wolf in the pack, he was tempting as sin even with a sore behind I'd let him have it any time, what I had come to learn about wolves was that nudity was the last thing they cared about unless you were mated, lustful looks of envy did not get their way onto you, they respected those boundaries.

Most of the teens were virgins as well like I once was, in every aspect of it, they liked to preserve themselves for their mates, I for one appreciated that I was my mates first and last, so if it were someone else in the pack I'm sure they would too, but there were some who didn't value that and got down and dirty, no one judged them though, family didn't judge you unless you betrayed the pack.

They were a close knit group, all of them and I was lucky to be part of it all, I waved at my mate when he looked up to find me drooling over him. "I see you eyefucking me." He spoke through the link. "I prefer long range appreciation but that works too, you are tempting as a beast after all." I sassed and he scoffed. "I see you need more pounding to be respectful in the morning." He growled and I chuckled.

"No pounding required I already serve on my knees don't I." I argued and he snickered. "We'll see how you be able to run that smart mouth of yours when I'm balls deep in you." He retorts along with a memory of him pounding me. "I'm going to be a good boy now." I asserted and he snorted. "Good, I have to let you go now, later my love." And the link was cut, the connection was open always but just on standby.

I decided to shower and give myself a waxing, though I loved my wolf hairy, I certainly didn't like myself like that, I didn't know why, I just didn't. As I got on with my bath I began to go through all that had happened these past few weeks, from falling in love with Train to finding out about wolves.

Life had basically been a roller coaster, I was grateful I survived whatever was thrown my way. My parents weren't in jail but Emric made sure they were far away from St Maine, my sister moved with them to wherever they had gone, and I was glad that I wouldn't be coming back home only to have my happy spirit dampened by the sight of the man who tried to kill me and the sister who never loved me.

I was happy with Train and what he did to them was payment enough for me, they would forever be seen without the perfection they craved and that was the revenge that I was happy with, though I had moved on I still reveled in the happiness that they were out of my life.

Along with the bad roller coaster came Fred the man who had my mate mentally breaking down, I never wanted to feel that sort of pain ever again, it wasn't my own but it felt as if it were, it pierced through and crushed me in depressing waves, no one should ever feel that way, and my mate had gone through that, I never wanted that for him.

So with the hope that Fred never returned we moved on with our lives, started afresh, and found a different path to take, Davey was gone, he had packed and left with his rogue alpha, Mrs. Ordell had put up her house for sale, and left Linden a letter, which he never opened and threw into the fire, she had walked away as well.

With her gone came the peace that Emric wanted for his mate, that Linden wouldn't have to deal with the fact that she had left him alone for years on end, basically abandoned him and when he found someone to love him and a home, she wanted him to stay which was hypocritical in a sense.

I sighed draining the bathtub, I had waxed, gave myself a perfect pedi and manicure along with taking time to heal my sore back, I felt refreshed and ready to take on the day, even if I had taken four hours in the bathroom.

The warriors were no longer training, and lunch was pretty much coming around soon, I decided to make it for my mate knowing he'll be coming up with the hunger of a beast. I changed into casual clothing and headed toward the kitchen, Linden had taught me how to use the appliances in the kitchen because somehow the way an ordinary stove was turned on, was not how the stove he installed in the kitchen worked, which was ridiculous but true.

I decided on steak lots and lots of steak and of course the rest of the food. "Hey babe, I'm back!" Train called out from the front door as I placed the mashed potatoes out. "Kitchen!" I yelled back, he wrapped me in his arms once he got to me and I held my breath. I kissed his cheek like he wanted but wouldn't let go till he groped me for more.

I kissed him till he was satisfied. "Now please go you stink, really bad." I exclaimed and he pouted. "What's a guy to do when I was running, fighting and training wolves on a grass and dirt field, all morning till early afternoon." He whined I placed a kiss on his cheek. "Go go shower, lunch is almost ready." He nodded happily and headed to our bedroom.

I had already adjusted to living with the Train in the suite, so I knew if we were to live together in an apartment, I would be okay with that, plus Train might be gay but all the qualities of a man were still intact and always out for show, which somehow I found attractive.

I finished making lunch and set the table for two, true to his nature, my mate came back wearing only a clean pair of boxers and socks with nothing else. He wasn't shy with his body and I could care less, he belonged to me anyway. "This is so good." He gobbled down his food as usual and I chuckled eating my own food, life was perfect for me now.

+++

LMJ

23.

Train.

"Argh I don't want to wake up." I groaned as my mate was pacing around the bedroom doing what in the world, I didn't know. "Seamonster wake up, its graduation, we need to be early, mom and dad are not taking us there, they're meeting us there." He shook me again and I whined even more.

"But I'm so comfortable." I mumbled clinging to the bed and he chuckled. "Is this any way to behave when you're finally saying goodbye to high school?" He questioned and I scoffed. "I said goodbye to damned high school half a year ago, this is just formality." I mumbled into the pillow inhaling the scent of the sea and flowers.

I wanted to find a way to propose to my mate but I couldn't find any other way, so I snuck the velvet box under his graduation gown along with pink roses and a note will you marry me, guess he didn't find it, I needed a new plan I guess.

"If you wake up now...you might see me naked." He teased and I whipped around immediately only to be disappointed, majorly disappointment, he was already fully clothed, but I could tear all his clothes off. I wickedly thought and woke up from the bed nude as the day I was born and stalked my prey.

My cock was bouncing with anticipation as we got closer to our prey. "No stay away from me, I'm not limping on stage!" My starfish yelled as he pushed me toward the bathroom. "Go in there, cold shower now." He ordered and like a good mate I groped him then went into the shower, the cold water helped cool me down.

After I cleaned up my clothes were ready for me all I did was lotion up and wear them. "Great, come have breakfast." Andie gestured to the table when I stood by the doorway. "When did you have time to make all this?" I question looking at the food arranged on the table. "I multi tasked, easy as baking pie." He replied innocently as I sat down for breakfast.

"Arent you mighty productive starfish." I teased and he blushed. "Am I now, thank you, kind sir." He replied with a grin as we are our breakfast. Somehow in all the mix of getting through graduation my mind drifted to Linden, today was the day the doctor said he would give birth after the error he made, so I was worried about him and I wished I could go see how he is, but I needed to get this whole school graduation over with.

"I'm finished, I'm gonna grab my wallet and your shoes, we'll be on our way." I exclaimed lifting my plate from the table, setting it by the kitchen sink. I headed toward our bedroom, got everything I wanted along with my mates shoes and we were on our way. "Oh Raziq is training the warriors today, shouldn't he be getting ready for the graduation?" My mate asked as we waved at Raziq by the grounds.

"No, when Linden and Emric graduated early he also graduated, he is the beta after all so he needed to help Emric, he's helped a lot with everything lately that's why we barely see him at times." I explained to my mate as we drove toward St Maine Academy, Raziq had been handling internal pack issues along with rogue activity or hunter activity which there is little to none, for us to focus on Tai's threat he had been holding some of the work for Emric.

Which he will probably do a lot more when my nephews are born, niece and nephew both but I really wanted nephews though, whichever was fine they would be spoilt rotten in any case. "Its started great, we don't have to stay here long." I muttered under my breath and my mate chuckled.

"Where have you two been, we've been here for a while." It wasn't my fault, for us to have seen Raziq training my mate had wanted to take pictures so it was. "It was his fault, he wanted to take photos, capture the moment as he put it." I dramatically exclaimed and my mother smacked my head. "Ouch mom, what did I do!" I whined whilst dad and my mate were already walking in front of us.

The large hall was slightly suffocating, though St Maine Academy didn't have a lot of students, the crowd had come from parents and students combined. The ceremony had begun indeed but the main reason why we were all gathered here had not begun. "Go find your seats, we'll be over there sweetheart." Mom instructed and I followed my mate when he pulled me along.

"I hate crowds." My starfish whined and I rubbed his back until we came up to two seats. "Did your parents somehow change my surname?" Andie asked and I mentally kicked myself obviously he didn't notice the ring or the will you marry me note under his gown, I wanted to play it cool but my wind lost its current.

"Yeah they did, they think never mind—." I cut myself off leading him to sit down. "The effort was appreciated sea monster but I want the whole deal, the whole shebang." He exclaimed and I turned to gasp as he was holding the box. "Like on one knee and shit, but I'm not good at that kind of stuff." I whined with a smile.

"I don't care so kneel for me." He ordered and I knelt in front of him. "Andrew Starfish Krest, I haven't known you for long but it feels like I've known you for a lifetime, you're my rock when times get tough, you're my solitude when life gets messed up and you're my love when I have none of my own left, I love you, and only you, will you let me be the one for you, in this life and the next, starfish marry me?" As I finished everyone was silent as was I.

"Yes, goddess yes!" He yelled and everyone clapped, the pack kids and parents cheered for us and I could see my mother wiping away tears. "Now that's a beautiful moment." I heard from the speakers as everyone had their attention on us. "I love you sea monster." He whispered and I kissed him earning more applause and wolf whistles.

"I'm in love with you Starfish and I don't want anybody else, and the world knows that, let's start our lives together from here on out, it's you and me hubby." I exclaimed and he wiped his tears away. "I'm all for that." He replied as my mother came to hug us and dad congratulated us.

"Train, you guys might want to get here, you're an uncle now and our parents are grandparents." Emric announced in my head and my eyes widened. "We have to go!" I yelled as I threw my mate over shoulder and ran, mom and dad were right behind. "Packhouse infirmary!" I yelled whilst buckling in my mate, sliding over the top of my car, and getting in.

I reversed and sped off toward the packhouse. "We're gonna beat you there honey!" My mother yelled as she hit the gas and sped off in front of us, I wasn't going to let her win so I stepped on it. "Woooooh!" My mate had a thing for fast cars. "I'm gonna beat you there mom!" I yelled passing her as we got onto pack territory. "Not on my watch Rookie!" She got past us again and got there first.

I got there closely behind her, unbuckled my mate, and ran with him over my shoulder. "What in the world of munchieland." Emric exclaimed watching us come running toward him. "I beat you, mom!" I yelled as we both skidded to a stop with our mates beside us.

"I have a crazy family." Emric mumbled shaking his head. "How is he, how are the babies?" Mom asked after we were calm. "They're all alright, Linden is resting now, he should wake up later, come see the babies." The alpha responded leading us to a room where two babies were inside two incubators.

"They have his hair, oh he looks just like his papa, definitely the alpha." Mom exclaimed holding one baby. "They're both very healthy boys." I mentally cheered when Emric added that bit of information. "I never wanna let him go." Andie cooed looking at the baby in his arms. "Emric, you and your mate made two good looking kids." Dad remarked cooing the babies as they were placed back on the tiny beds and incubators.

"Thanks, dad." He replied as we walked out, two wolves came and guarded the door, I didn't question it, I just knew he was an alpha with newly born pups. Today had been a great day, we had more to celebrate as we wolves always found reason to celebrate but this time the reason was valid to a point, I was a fucking uncle and an engaged man.

+++

Epilogue.

Ben Platt ~ Grow as we go.

A Human's Desires.

Train.

Today was the day, the day we started a life away from my family, from all that I loved, I wondered if that's what I wanted, could I survive being away for so long. I was on a tailspin literally and I didn't know if my mind would ever calm down.

The bags had already been packed and ready to go, letters had been posted, we had already moved a few of our things to the apartment in Algiers, all that was left was to go there and start our college life as a married couple. I sighed picking up my phone and texting my brother, I wanted to talk to him before I decided to leave.

He was at the packhouse so I walked down to his office and walked right in, the gibberish of the twins had me smiling, he was on babysitting duty today. "Are you all packed?" Em asked with a smile but I didn't reciprocate it. "You're having cold feet huh." He exclaimed and I wasn't surprised that he knew I had cold feet about going.

He always knew me, read me like an open book and when we were younger it bugged the hell out of me. "I am, should I really be leaving you when you're like this." I gestured to him rocking London the little baby alpha whilst signing documents. "It seems like I'm leaving you with a burden that I could've lightened if I was here." I argued taking Luciano from his crib and rocking him.

"Train we already had this conversation before, mom, dad, Linden their dad, Emma, Terric, Raziq and junior are all here to help, you've wanted to do this with your mate for a while now, you guys need to experience stuff away from the safety of home, to explore on your own." Emric contended and I knew he was right but it didn't make me feel better.

"I know it's just it's hard okay, all I've know this whole year is that this is home, and I'm scared to leave." I confessed changing the way I was holding Luca. "That's the point of every new endeavor Train, it tests your courage, and bravery, mentally and physically, you knew leaving wasn't going to be easy and staying would just make you stagnant, this is a chance to discover yourself even further with your husband by your side, it's going to be okay." He comforted and I took in every word he said.

"And Train, you're only a four hour flight away from here, it's not that far, it will be like you never left, Linden and I will visit, and you'll come here for holidays and any other moment that strikes you to just come home, like dad always says home is where the people who fill your heart with love are, so when you go there with Andrew you already have a piece of home beside you." Emric smiled gently as I placed sleeping Luca back on the crib and hugged him.

"There there brother, you're going to be fine." I was going to be fine, I knew that but I was sure as hell that I was going to miss my parents, brother, my nephews and my best friend, I was really going to miss him. "I'm gonna miss you." I mumbled and he chuckled. "I'm obviously going to miss you too, who will defend me when my mate is out for my balls." He chortled and we both laughed.

"I'm sure if you convince him about their particular use he won't chop them off." I asserted and he chuckled lowly not wanting to wake up London, the baby alpha had pipes and always out for mischief, I could see a lot of me and Em in the twins, they had each other's backs but we also got into a whole lot of trouble.

"I'm gonna finish packing, Andie should be back with my mom by now." I announced and the alpha nodded as I left him to take care of his kids in silence whilst signing off documents, he had become a fine alpha, maybe he was right, I needed to take my own path, discover what I like, explore a world beyond safety blanket of home, with my husband by my side.

When I come back I could easily help Emric, I would be more efficient and I would've found my own way into the world, like my brother had, he didn't become alpha because he was born with the claim, he earned the right to be alpha by making his own path in the world and getting recognized in his own way.

I wanted to do what he had encouraged me to do, and make him proud. "Hey starfish, how was shopping with mom?" I asked entering our bedroom where my mate was changing and packing. "You ready to go?" He questioned with a smile and I nodded. I no longer had cold feet about going, I was ready to face the world and become an admirable man for my mate and for my family and someday my own kids.

I didn't want to disappoint them and myself so I was going to dive in headfirst into this new endeavor, my head was not going to get a concussion, I was diving into the deep end. "I had cold feet but I talked to mom, and she made me realize that going to college after all that's happened this year was the best thing for us, we needed to do this, she also made me promise that

I would excel with my art and make her even more so proud." My starfish explained and I hugged him.

"We can do this baby, we've faced worse and she was right, we're going to Algiers and we're going to excel, for us mostly and for our family, that's why I no longer have cold feet, I found my footing again and we shouldn't worry, we have each other, as Emric said, we're only a four hour flight away from home, we can always come back." I reassured my mate and kissed him.

"You ready guys?" Dad asks as we were now packed and ready to go by the door. "Yeah we are." I replied and he winked at me with his signature smile, goddess I was going to miss that smile. We made it downstairs as the pack members bid us farewell and wished us luck, they were truly family and I wouldn't have it otherwise.

"Come on the flight is in an hour." Mom announced and we got into their Jeep, Emric and the kids were in his car, which he was driving and the babies at the back with their dad, I was going to miss babysitting my nephews. "You're going to miss those two huh." Andie remarked as he laid his head on my bicep.

"Im going to miss them like crazy." I confessed as my hard brushed up on his back. "We have break, we can always come back and see them, plus video chats, I'm sure we won't miss a thing." He suggested and I agreed with him, we could always watch them grow as we go.

We arrived at the airport thirty minutes later, Linden was a crying mess as he held onto me. "I can't believe this is happening, I'm going to miss you guys." He sniffled as I held him in an embrace. "Come on you big baby we won't be that far." Andie teased but that only made it worse. "But you'll still be far." He whined again until Emric intervened.

"Babe you have to let him go, you know got to, but he'll be back and you'll milk his time for all it's worth, right." Linden nodded wiping away his tears. "I'm gonna miss you peanut and you too starfish." He mumbled and we both hugged him. "Love you mama munchie." I replied as he drew back to stand by his mate.

"Just know I'm so proud of you, I will never be anything other than proud of you." Mom hugged us after handing London to Emric, I chuckled as she cried not wanting to let go of both of us. "Mom you have to let us go, we love you mom, we always will." I reassured and she chuckled whilst letting go.

"Be careful, call once in a while and always remember home is where we are and we'll never leave you." Dad stated proudly like a father and Andie hugged him as he ruffled my hair. "Go." It was Emric who spoke. "Love you, brother." I spoke through the link. "Love you too Train." He replied as we made our way to the boarding gate.

I didn't want to look back because if I did I would turn back and never want to leave, my mate and I had to do this, but we would always be back. "And Linden, don't worry, I will be back before you know it."